AUGMENTED

REALITY

By James Jackson

Printed by Amazon

Cover Design by Jason Williams

ISBN: 978-1-941-590-21-8

Author's Works

Terran Chronicles Universe

First Contact
Johnny's Jaunt
Discovery
Pythos
Joe's Notes: Gamin Technology
Colony
Jie's World
Emma's Legacy
Alliance
End of Times
Voknor Diaries
Sharz Affect

Other Works

Mamluk
America – At a Crossroads

Dedication

To the lessons of the past; may they teach us to live in the present, while allowing us to dream of the future.

Acknowledgements

To Jairis, John, Michael, and the many others who follow my writing, I thank you all for your constant support.

A special thank you goes to Shannon and Jeff, who reviewed, then edited this story. I greatly appreciate the vast amount of time, energy, and effort, they contribute. I would not be the writer I am today, without their ongoing support.

Another person I must thank is my longtime friend, Jason. His website design work, book cover art, along with his dedication and support is greatly appreciated.

Table of Contents

Preface

Humanity's future is as exciting as it is terrifying. Augmented reality has been around for some time, thanks to the advent of digital technology. It is now part of our everyday lives; televised sports have captions and information laid out, as if on the playing field. Smartphones allow us to capture and battle virtual creatures as if they existed right next to us, but in a plane of existence beyond our natural ability to see, feel, or sense. The possibilities for this technology seem endless, but what if the government took control? What would our future be like?

"Reality is merely an illusion, albeit a very persistent one." – Albert Einstein

"Appearances are often deceiving." - Aesop

I hereby welcome you all to 'Augmented Reality'.

This is a work of fiction, or is this our ultimate destiny?
I hope you, the reader, enjoy this as much as I have enjoyed writing it.

James Jackson

Chapter One - Utopia

Joe stares at the pavement, baffled. He frowns as he gazes around. He had stumbled on something, but there is nothing on the ground, nor is the pavement damaged. The slab of pearl white concrete is in pristine condition, just like everything else in the capital. Still staring down, his frown deepens as he wonders what had almost tripped him.

"SCORE!"

He jerks his head up at the unexpected noise.

The loud announcement, followed by even louder cheering, interrupts his thoughts. He looks across the street at the side of a large building, one playing the afternoon game between the Paragons and the Mech-fits. The Paragons, the team his city, Canfield, supports, just scored a touchdown. He stops and watches the game for a moment, then upon noticing that his team leads by eighteen points, resumes his walk. He knows they will win, they have a convincing lead.

He looks up and down the street at the perfectly manicured footpath; each side lined with lush, well-kept, grass. A few shrubs dot the grass patches every now and then, as do some flower arrangements. Small electric vehicles quietly hum back and forth along the road, the blacktop beneath the gleaming vehicles shimmering in the sunlight. The other side is identical, right down to the neatly kept grass. The contrasting colors are neat, orderly, and relaxing; Joe smiles as he continues on his way.

The vehicles' occupants are engrossed in one thing or another, as they are driven to their destinations. Some stare down at devices in their hands, while the more affluent have the latest in holo-projectors, with which they watch news casts, play games, or communicate with friends.

Joe sighs as he moves on, mumbling, "I'll never be able to afford a transit vehicle."

He continues his walk to the local park, where he sits upon a wooden bench, and watches the idyllic scene. Birds chirp in the trees, or swoop down to the sparkling blue pond, while squirrels and chipmunks vie for the nuts on the ground beneath massive trees. Joe is proud to live in the capital; crime is virtually nonexistent, while living conditions are the best they have ever been. There are no beggars, unemployment is almost unheard of, and wages are more than enough to live on. A few luxury items, like personal transport vehicles and penthouse living quarters, are beyond the reach of most people. But all in all, the average person is able to travel, explore the arts, or play sports.

"Joe!"

"Henry." Joe replies politely as a man his age, mid-thirties, approaches.

"Did you see that touchdown?" Henry shouts as he punches the air enthusiastically, "Woohoo!"

"I did!" Joe grins, then adds, "We're kicking their butts, again!"

Henry glances around as he sits next to Joe, then unexpectedly, he lowers his voice, "Any truth to the rumor that the Central Authority is cutting back on fixers?"

Joe fidgets nervously. Negative talk about the Central Authority is dangerous, even something as mundane as employment. He ponders his answer as he watches a squirrel run up the side of a tree, its mouth filled by a large seed pod.

"They must have enough." Joe shrugs, "I never see any of them working anyway, everything is perfect."

Henry's eyes flicker as he leans closer to Joe, and whispers so low that he is hard to understand, "They're replacing the fixers with machines!"

Joe listens to the words, unconcerned, then chuckles, "Okay, and?"

Henry gulps, "You don't get it do you? The Central Authority controls the machines, but they rely on the fixers to keep them maintained. By replacing the people with auto-fixers, we'll have machines, fixing machines."

Joe grins innocently as he replies, "What's wrong with that?"

Henry's face twitches as he mutters, "No one knows how half the machines work anymore. Machines make and repair each other; and soon they'll run everything! Who repairs the systems they can't?"

"What systems?" Joe frowns, "Besides, we haven't had a power outage in decades, plus, with our weather control systems, damaging storms of the past, are just that, in the past. There is nothing to repair, everything just works perfectly."

Henry grabs Joe as he stammers, "Listen to me, these auto-fixers are something new, we need to know how to fix things. We…"

"Can I be of assistance?" Interrupts an auto-cop from behind them.

Joe stares at the tall humanoid-looking machine with dread, then says, "Oh no, we're okay." Its super-quiet electric motors had allowed it to approach, unnoticed.

The machine detects a change in Joe's bio-scan, then determines that he is frightened, and not trying to hide anything. Henry's bio-scan, however, tells a different story. The man is unstable, and therefore a risk to society.

Henry stands as he says, "Well, I'll be off then." He takes two steps away before he is brought down by an electric shock from the auto-cop.

Three more auto-cops approach, seemingly out of nowhere. Joe has only ever seen one before, and it was being transported. He has never heard of so many being in the same place at the same time, ever.

Henry grunts strangely as he wriggles on the ground. He gets to his knees, points a device at the closest auto-cop and fires a beam of light at the machine. Rising, he then sprints away.

Joe is stunned and does not have to be told by the other auto-cops to remain where he is. He could not run if he wanted to, besides why would he? And where could he go? The Central Authority knows everything. He stares at the immobile auto-cop in total disbelief, while two others pursue Henry.

"Follow me." Orders the remaining auto-cop.

Joe is scared for his safety, and afraid of what will happen to him as he trails behind the machine. He then realizes that from his earliest days, he was taught that only bad people had to fear the authorities, which picks up his spirits. He is not the bad person, Henry is!

For the first time in his life he rides inside a personal transit vehicle, and not one of the long tubes, crammed with people. He looks at the machine next to him, reflecting on Henry's comments. As they move along the street he recognizes a neighbor, and waves. She looks back, but does not seem to notice him, nor does she acknowledge his waving. They zip along the streets, faster than the few other vehicles, until they arrive at a huge building, where they enter an underground parking station.

Stepping out, Joe is surprised to see dozens of auto-cops, along with numerous vehicles. He follows the auto-cop to a small room, where he sits in one of two large comfortable chairs, and waits. The room is almost as large as his apartment's main room, but that's where the similarities end. Grey tiles and white walls are testimony to the utilitarian nature of the place, and while his apartment is filled with all sorts of entertainment gadgets, this room only has the two chairs in it.

Joe twiddles his thumbs as he waits, his apprehension returning. Although he believes he is innocent of any crime, he does not know anyone who has been to this building in the city. He glances around as the minutes pass, fears mounting.

After what feels like an eternity, someone steps into the room; a tall man wearing a white laboratory coat. The man taps on a hand-held device as he questions, "Joe? Joe Roberts of third sector, division two, apartment nineteen?"

Joe stammers, "Uh, um. Yes, yes. That's, that's me."

"Good." The man replies, sitting in the remaining chair. He stares at Joe for a moment, evaluating him, then states, "My name is Doctor Liang, and I am here to qualify your relationship with Henry."

Joe is baffled by the statement, and replies, "I don't have a relationship with him."

"Sure you do." Liang presses, "You were conversing with him. You know who he is."

"Oh," Joe replies quickly, then adds, "I thought you meant," He pauses, then mumbles, "never mind."

Doctor Liang continues, "How long have you known Henry?"

"A few years," Joe replies, then upon seeing Liang's stern expression, says, "Six years. I think it's been six years."

"How did you meet?" Liang continues as he taps on his device.

"It was through work. We both trade in the public markets." Joe replies, then upon seeing that the Doctor is waiting for more details, he continues. "We co-worked a few large accounts." Under the Doctor's continuing stern stare, he mumbles, "Long-term stuff."

Liang glances at his hand-held, then states more than questions, "You both work for the same company, Transit Tax Dividends, on X block."

"Yes!" Joe exclaims, surprised by the doctor's knowledge, then he suddenly he feels silly, of course the doctor knows everything, he is part of the Central Authority.

The doctor puts his hand-held down, leans forward, then says, "If you wish to go home soon, then I will require detailed answers to my questions." he stares sternly at Joe, then questions, "Is that understood?"

Joe gulps, "Yes sir."

Liang's questions are varied, encompassing many aspects of Joe's life, from his daily habits to his occasional vacation. With each response, Liang checks Joe's galvanic response, eventually determining that he is indeed, an innocent bystander. He taps his device as he wonders if he should send Joe to mental health, for a memory wipe.

Doctor Liang stands, then instructs, "Wait here."

Joe tries to smile as he meekly replies, "Of course." The session has been quite draining and left him feeling numb.

Liang makes his way to an observation room, where he nods to another man who has been watching.

"He is either the smartest subvert in the dissident movement, or an idiot!" Arnold proclaims loudly.

Arnold is pushy, someone who uses his burly size and bravado, to get his own way. He is also an investigator of subvert activity, which provides him with considerable influence within the Central Authority.

"He is neither." Doctor Liang replies, "If you watch closely, and listen carefully, you'll see that Henry initiated the entire conversation."

"Yes, I see that!" Arnold snaps, irritated at being told the obvious. "But," he presses as he steps closer to Liang, "it was Joe who chose the meeting area." He folds his arms and grins, as if he has just solved the case with his proclamation.

Liang shakes his head as he replies with a chuckle, one which infuriates Arnold, "Joe has been going to that park for years, if he really is a subvert, he would be avoiding that place like the plague."

Arnold's eyes flicker in annoyance as he realizes that Doctor Liang is right. He reluctantly admits, "That would be a bad place for Subverts to meet. There are many other areas of the city which are monitored with less diligence."

Liang paces back and forth as he suggests an idea which has been on his mind, "I think we should send Joe back, without a memory wipe, to see what happens."

Arnold's jaw drops at the idea, "That is preposterous. What if he talks?"

"What of it?" Liang replies with a shrug, "He may even attract Subverts, they're sure to wonder what Henry wanted with him, just like us."

"No one will talk to him now, the Subverts will know he's been here." Arnold states bluntly.

"Pull the active monitors then." Liang suggests.

Arnold is floored by the brazen idea, and snorts, "Do you have any idea how dangerous the Subverts could be to our way of living if they ever…" he stops talking, and stares at Liang as an idea of his own comes to mind.

Liang is confused by Arnold's behavior, and remains quiet as the man paces back and forth with his hands behind his back, muttering to himself.

Arnold stops, looks straight at Liang then exclaims, "You're a genius!"

Liang blinks in surprise, "I am?"

"Yes." Arnold states with a grin. "We'll let Joe go without wiping his memory, and we won't monitor him. In fact, we'll disable his chip's tracking mode."

Doctor Liang is confused, "But without the tracking feature, even we won't know where he goes?"

"And the first time a subvert scans him, they will be surprised, and I'm sure they'll want to question him." Arnold states with confidence.

"Right…" Liang slowly agrees, then scowls as he questions, "And that helps us, how, exactly?"

Arnold grins as he replies, "Joe isn't a subvert. He's an honest citizen, a worker and contributor to our society. And now he's going to lead us to them."

"But without the tracking…" Liang begins, then grins as he realizes what Arnold is planning. "Oh my!" He exclaims, "I know what you're thinking."

The two men discuss in detail what they plan to do, both knowing that if their idea fails, they could be the ones being investigated. However, the rewards far outweigh the risks, and thus they agree to take the chance. This is after all, a rare opportunity.

Joe looks up nervously as the doctor enters the room. He has been alone with his thoughts and fears for some time.

Doctor Liang smiles pleasantly as he approaches Joe, and says, "Mister Roberts, there has been a huge mistake. He holds up his hand-held as he continues, "After reviewing the auto-cop video, we have confirmed your story fully, and apologize for this inconvenience."

Joe opens his mouth to speak, but does not know what to say.

Arnold watches from an observation room, grinning as he relishes in this once in a lifetime opportunity. A truly innocent person, one who never even knew about Subverts, may well lead to their eradication.

Liang frowns, as planned, and then hesitantly asks, "Is there anything we can do to compensate you for your troubles?"

Joe swallows hard, then says, "Can I get a ride home please?" he shrugs as he adds, "I'm not even sure where I am."

"How about we loan you a vehicle for a short time, say a month or two?" Liang offers.

Joe stares wide-eyed as he stammers, "I'm… I'm… I'm, not sure if my apartment is allotted a parking spot." His mind is racing over the idea of a personal vehicle.

Liang nods, and pauses as if thinking, then says, "Well, how about we upgrade your apartment to one with parking?" He pauses again, then continues, "How does sector one sound?"

Joe swallows hard, then with his mind still reeling, replies sullenly, "But, my job does not qualify me for sector one living."

Arnold shakes his head as he watches. He mutters to himself, "Joe is such a well-conditioned citizen. We're offering more than he could ever have hoped to achieve, and he is still finding things to worry about." He grins as he watches Liang pace the room, as if he is pondering what to do.

Doctor Liang sighs, then taps on his hand-held for a few moments. "Ah ha!" he exclaims, causing Joe to jump. With a grin he states, "There is a vacancy on E block for a private market manager."

Joe stares blankly, then softly replies, "E block, private markets! Oh my."

Liang holds a finger poised over his hand-held as he asks, "So, is that a yes?"

"Yes. Yes!" Joe replies a little louder than he expected, his excitement building.

Arnold grins from his vantage point, then rubs his hands together as he relishes in the way they have easily manipulated Joe. He is still ginning when he walks to a console, and authorizes Joe's relocation and job change, all earmarked under the umbrella of 'special projects'. He also details how Doctor Liang approached him with the idea, just in case things do not work out as planned; he will need a scapegoat.

Doctor Liang retires to his office, where he too documents the day's events. But he has another agenda, and quickly sends a few discrete messages. Once done, he erases all records of his communications, then puts his hands behind his head and leans back in his chair as he wonders what will happen next.

Meanwhile, in another office, a third man is secretly watching events unfold exactly as he had anticipated. He takes a deep breath as he slides away from his computer, where Joe's profile fills the screen. His mind races over numerous possibilities, and with each one he considers how to react. He closes his eyes as he spins around in his chair, muttering, "Who guards the guards?"

Chapter Two – The Resort

Joe sits in his vehicle, enjoying the scenery as he travels to the city's outskirts. He has only been in his new position for a few weeks, and already has earned a three-day vacation to an exclusive holiday resort. His new position also affords him the luxury of keeping his vehicle. He is still surprised by the turn of events, but then, his ability to maneuver stocks, for profit, is earning him quite a reputation with his superiors. The steady hum of the vehicle's electric motors, along with the warmth of the sun, causes him to doze off.

Arnold has been watching Joe's work with great interest. He is astonished to learn that Joe really does have talent in dabbling with the intricacies of the stock market. He had expected to have to bail him out and is pleasantly surprised when he learns that Joe is legitimately increasing his client's portfolio values. Joe's vacation is another surprise, and further proof of his abilities, but as for letting him keep the vehicle, that was planned for from the start. It is after all, how they will keep tabs on his general whereabouts.

Joe smiles as the vehicle stops. He waits for the door to open, allowing him to exit. Leaving the items he packed, he gets out and walks through the double front doors of the building. He stops and gawks, amazed. The entryway is a vast open area; stone pillars hold aloft the high ceiling, while granite flooring stretches as far as he can see. Trees grow in massive pots along the walls, resting on either side of tall, drape-lined, windows. The area smells fresh, like spring. Joe closes his eyes and takes in a deep breath, relishing in the experience.

"Sir, may I help you?" The soft, polite voice interrupts Joe's thoughts.

Opening his eyes, he sees a petite young woman in front of him. Her youthful face, high cheek bones, radiant smile, and sparkling amber eyes are a surprise. He is instantly enamored; he has never seen anyone so beautiful in his life. She is wearing a dark blue shirt, one with a deep V-neck, showing her shapely form, along with a short, matching skirt. Judging by the emblems and style, this is the uniform for the employees. Even so, she could be a model for any one of a dozen circulations, Joe considers as he gazes at the beautiful woman.

"Ah, yes." Joe finally replies, after staring for far too long. He swallows nervously as he glances away, adding, "I have a room booked, for three days."

She giggles, then tilts her head coyly as she replies, "My name is Miranda. Welcome to Holiday Resort Fiesta. If you would follow me please, we can get your *suite* organized at the main desk."

Joe follows the attractive woman, drifting in the wake of her lovely perfume. Her skirt swishes atop her long, tanned and fit, legs. He quickly looks away, embarrassed by his own thoughts. It is not like he has never had the company of a woman before, but still, Miranda is like no woman he has ever seen.

Her hips swing as she leads Joe to a large desk, which appears to be made of solid wood. She steps around to the other side, where she grabs a hand-held computer, and begins tapping on its screen.

Joe frowns in confusion as she hands him a plastic door-key, a pamphlet, and a card. He asks curiously, "How do you know who I am?"

"You're Joe Roberts?" Miranda states more than asks, then says, "We've been expecting you."

"Oh," he replies, then as he stares into her attractive eyes, adds, "this is beautiful."

Miranda lifts her eyebrows teasingly, then asks, "Is there *anything* I can do for you?"

"Ah, um," he stammers, then as he blushes, clumsily asks, "Can I call later?"

"You sure can!" She replies, enthusiastically nodding.

Joe walks away from the desk, not sure what just happened. He has completely forgotten his luggage.

"You have to try the health spa," she calls out after him, "it's part of your package, and well worth the time."

Joe turns to her, then smiles as he replies, "Okay, I will."

Miranda responds suggestively, "You would have time before dinner, and be fresh and relaxed for the evening."

Joe swallows hard as rarely entertained thoughts come to mind. He answers as casually as he can, "I'll do just that."

Her radiant smile beams, her only response.

Turning away, Joe follows the directions to his room, where he steps inside and stops, stunned by the sight. He has never seen such displays of opulence. The entry is paved in natural grey stone, while dark wood covers the walls. A large closet, almost the size of a small room really, is for coats and jackets, with space for shoes and other clothing that requires hanging.

20

He takes a few steps, then stops when he reaches the plush grey carpet. On the left is a kitchen, complete with a tall, wide, work area, and all manner of appliances. A large couch, with cushions arranged neatly on it, rests alongside the right-hand wall. An ornate wooden coffee table occupies the space between the couch and a monstrous wall screen. Ahead of him, large, closed, blue-grey drapes hang from near the ceiling, dropping almost all the way to the floor. A small table rests against the wall near the lounge, upon which sits an exquisite light. A comfortable looking chair is slid under the table's edge.

Joe walks up to the coffee table, then runs his hand along the table-top, feeling the grain's texture. He whistles as he exclaims, "Real wood. Damn!"

He leaves the items Miranda handed him on the table, then strides to the drapes and opens them. The view is majestic and does not look real. He opens the sliding door and steps out onto the patio. A cool wind, mixed with the scent of pine trees, brushes his face. Beyond the forest, and the slow-moving river, snow covered mountain peaks poke through a layer of fluffy clouds. He does not recall seeing the mountains as he travelled, but he pays little heed to the matter.

Stepping back inside, he slides the door shut, and then checks the bedroom. His forgotten luggage is resting on the enormous bed, waiting for him. Three puffy pillows line the bedhead, while an animal skin adorns the wooden floor. Leaning down, he rubs the tiger's fur, then feeling odd irregularities, he lifts an edge, and frowns. Real animal hides are horrifically expensive, and not something he has ever seen before, nor did he ever expect to in his lifetime. He walks to the closed drapes, and peeks through them at the same magnificent view of the mountains. He can almost feel the breeze and smell the trees.

Joe looks around as he wonders where the bathroom is. Noticing a pair of French-doors, he grins as he steps through them. He was expecting something impressive, and yet is still floored by the extravagance. Gold fittings are everywhere, from the spa bath, to the two-person shower, along with the double sink. An ornate toilet occupies a recess that appears to have been carved from a single block of granite.

Stunned, he returns to the bed where he unpacks his few belongings. He places his clothes into the drawers or hangs them up in the walk-in closet. Walking to the lounge, he picks up the corporate card, and opens it. 'All meals and entertainment are for your pleasure. Enjoy.'

He has no idea what he should do, so he follows Miranda's suggestion, and heads to the health spa. Another pretty young woman meets him, but she does not exude the same aura as Miranda. Joe is led to a full immersion spa-treatment room, where, following instructions, he undresses when she leaves, then steps into a special mix of warm water and cleansing agents. He puts on a face-mask, then closes his eyes and lays back in the full-length bath. Breathing through the nose piece he relaxes, completely engulfed in the watery mix. The experience literally tingles his senses, while the deep cleansing properties of the warm liquid open his pores. Quite a while later, a bell chimes, indicating that it is time for him to get out. He slops all over as he makes his way to the shower, where he washes the remnants of the cleansing mix off his body.

Next, he wraps a towel around his waist and walks to a massage room. He is surprised to see Miranda waiting for him and is too dumbfounded to say anything.

Smiling, she says, "Please lay face down, your masseuse will be with you shortly."

Curiosity gets the better of Joe, so he asks, 'What are you doing here? Is this part of your normal duties?"

When there is no answer, he looks up; she is gone. A muscular man is in her place. The man grins as he instructs, "Relax."

Joe is not sure if he liked the massage, he feels as though *mister muscles* enjoyed torturing him as opposed to relaxing him. He stares at the glass of water, the third since the massage, and downs it. He can still hear the muscle-bound man telling him to drink plenty of water. The final leg of the treatment is a facial, which includes an amazing shave, coupled with a manicure and pedicure.

Instead of dressing in his earlier clothes, he takes an offered robe, and walks to his room. Though his clothes were clean that morning, he wants a fresh outfit for the evening. Arriving at his room, he finds a note has been slid under his door. 'Enjoy your dinner, I will see you later tonight - Miranda'.

Joe turns the note over and over as he wonders why she is interested in him, then with a sigh, decides that she is probably toying with him. He considers if she wants money, then chuckles. It would be easy enough to check his financial value, which he realizes, is probably quite meager compared to most who come to the resort.

Sorting through his few clothes, he selects his best outfit; black striped, grey dress pants, along with a long sleeve, crisp-blue shirt. His black shoes are freshly polished, which does not surprise him, considering the treatment he has received thus far. He dresses, then decides to have an early dinner.

As Joe walks to the dining hall, a man approaches and grins as he says, "I thought I recognized you. Joe, right?"

Joe is perplexed as he replies, "I'm sorry, I don't remember you."

"Gordon's the name, stocks the game." The man replies with exaggerated flair as he opens his arms.

Joe's jaw drops; Gordon's ability to predict stock fluctuations is legendary. Rumor has it that he rarely attends meetings, or even shows up at his office. "You're Gordon. The Gordon!" He exclaims, astonished by being in the presence of the man so few see.

Gordon holds his hand out as he says, "Join me for dinner, we can swap stories."

Joe lowers his gaze as he replies, "Oh, I think you've mistaken me for someone else. I'm sure you have important people to have dinner with."

"Nonsense." Gordon states bluntly, "I would love it if you would join me."

"Okay." Joe replies, thinking that it would be an insult not to eat with the man he has heard so much about.

Joe follows Gordon to a lavish table, one far larger than needed for the two of them. The wait staff quickly and efficiently set the table for two, doing so in such a way that neither man notices them working.

Moments later, both men are sipping on mountain-fresh water as they review an extensive menu.

Gordon taps the table as he asks, "Do you think the lobster tail or the steak? I can't decide."

Joe has been staring at the menu, then feeling out of place quietly asks, "There are no prices. I'm not even sure I can afford anything in this place!" Most of the items on the menu are things he has never seen offered at the places he eats, but like many people, he has heard of them, most of them anyway.

Gordon laughs heartily, then replies, "This is your first corporate vacation, I should have realized."

Joe shifts uncomfortably, and lowers his gaze as he looks around, trying to come up with an excuse to leave.

Gordon leans forward, softly places a hand on Joe's arm, and says, "I apologize. I was not making fun of you, but rather the corporation. They'll do anything to save money. They didn't tell you all meals are covered, did they?"

Recalling the card, Joe relaxes, then says, "They did, I just didn't think it meant for this place too!"

Gordon motions for a waiter, then grinning widely says, "I would like the lobster, as will my friend. Oh, and a bottle of ice wine."

As the waiter leaves, Gordon nods to Joe, and says, "And if we don't like it, we'll order the steak!"

Joe frowns as he recalls something from work, then his jaw drops as he says, "I just transferred ice wine stocks, giving a client a sixteen percent gain in three weeks."

Lowering his voice, Gordon states, "An impressive gain. How did you do that?" He asks, inquisitively.

"I noticed that the local harvests were yielding poor results, but wineries further out were reporting bumper crops. I simply timed the shift in confidence, buying and selling at the right time." Joe shrugs his shoulders as he adds, "In reality, I got lucky."

Gordon shakes his head as he replies, "No, you noticed a shift in the market, and capitalized on it."

The pair shares more trade stories, many of which amaze Joe. Along the way Gordon shares, or lets slip, a few of his trade secrets. Either way, Joe does his best to pay attention.

A few more guests join the dining hall, but not as many as Joe expected. They talk as evening rolls on, eventually leaving five empty bottles of ice wine on the table. Joe struggles to make his way to his room, and once there, he splashes water on his face in an attempt to sober up.

A timid knock at the door brings him to his senses. He dries his face, then stumbles to the door, and opens it.

Miranda stands before him, in tight jeans, and a loose top. She laughs as she says, "Oh my, you've had your fill, haven't you? Gordon is such a naughty boy, spoiling all my fun!"

Taking Joe's hand, she leads him to the bed, where no matter how hard he tries to stay awake, he is unable to. Once he is sound asleep, Miranda begins. It does not take her long, as she is well practiced in her duties.

The Mountain

Joe stares at the frozen landscape in bewilderment. He has no clear recollection of how he got to where he is, nor did he know that such a place existed. An enormous mountain dominates the view to his left, while a massive wall of rocks obscures his view to the right. Between these, a jagged dam-wall has formed from frozen waters. A few people are milling around, also watching the wintery scene. Joe shakes his head as he tries to understand what is going on.

He frowns as dim memories of a vehicle traveling along a mountainside road come to mind. His frown deepens as he pulls at the memory fragments, digging deeper, then feels a chill as he recalls being the operator of the vehicle, something he did not know could be done, let alone by him. What this has to do with where he is, baffles him.

Suddenly aware of how cold it is, he glances down at his bare feet. He wiggles his dirty toes in the snow, and grins stupidly as the light snow puffs around his feet. He notices a pair of boots in front of him, his boots, but he does not know how he knows this, and frowns once more. He bends down, reaching for the boots, causing his glasses to slip off his face. Joe watches as the glasses seem to fall in slow motion and land on the snow-covered ground. Up until this moment he was not aware that he was wearing them. A man steps back, almost crushing them.

"Watch it!" Joe snaps as he snatches his glasses and boots, then finding a thick sock tucked into each boot, puts them on.

A deep rumbling emanates from the majestic mountain, followed by an avalanche of snow, ice, smashed trees, and other debris. Joe watches as it slides behind the distant wall. The avalanche continues unabated; the volume soon exceeds the height of the wall, and yet, instead of spilling over, continues to build up behind it, forming a new wall, one at least three times taller. Steady vibrations crack the ground nearby, revealing a wide, slow-moving river.

Many of the people continue to stare, while a few others climb onto small machines. They start up noisily, and are even louder as they roar off; the people on them hunkering down behind short windshields. Joe watches as the strange machines sink into the water, yet keep going forward. They skim across the icy river, their wide single-tracks spray churned up water, ice, and snow, in their wakes. Water laps at the long footplates, threatening to breach their narrow, raised edges.

Joe's fingers play with an object in his pocket, a key! He takes it out, then stares at another of these machines, a bright red one sitting on the ground next to him. He does not question why he did not see it before, and straddles the machine. The controls are oddly familiar to him.

A young girl runs his way, her long brown hair swinging behind her as she rushes toward him. She is nine or ten years old, and surprises him when, with an air of familiarity, she asks, "Are we leaving?"

"Climb on." Joe hears himself say, then as the avalanche threatens to spill over the dam, he shouts to the others, "Get out of here you damn fools!"

The girl climbs on behind Joe, then holds him tight as he starts the machine and roars off. They travel along the river's edge, avoiding the churning waters when they can. Coming upon an opening in the rock wall, Joe makes for it, and stops. He stares with disbelief at the sight; they are atop an impossibly high mountain, not the safe area he had hoped to discover. A vertical cliff plummets into the clouds below. Other mountain peaks jut out of the clouds in the distance, while above them are clear blue skies.

"LOOK!" The girl screams as she points toward the dam.

They watch as the avalanche succumbs to its weight, and tips over the wall, crashing down. The impact drives up the icy coating on the water, creating waves of flotsam, which head their way.

Joe fumbles for the key, struggling in his panic to get it into the machine's lock. He does not recall taking the key out. As he succeeds, a heavy-set woman stumbles into view.

She breathlessly begs, "Please take me."

Joe stares at the water's edge which is already becoming choppy, then glances back at the cliff. Adrenaline rushes through his veins at the realization that if they remain where they are, they will be washed off the cliff, and fall into the oblivion below.

"Get on!" Joe instructs with more confidence than he feels.

The weight of the three of them threatens to sink the machine as it crosses the choppy, murky expanse. Joe twists it left and right as he attempts to avoid the larger floating obstacles. He is mostly successful, but feels the girl's fingers dig into his ribs each time something strikes them, spinning them around.

As they sink deeper, Joe shouts, "Hold on tight!" He then applies full power.

His fingers begin to slip off the handlebars as they lurch forward, and although the footplates dip below the water, they continue toward the far bank. The river swells around, pushing them sideways downstream, then, miraculously, the front of the vehicle's track finds purchase on the muddy riverbank. The rear of the track flings great gouts of dirt as Joe pushes the machine to its limit, its engine roaring in protest, yet they are unable to climb the slippery slope.

Joe reduces power, then glances over his shoulder, instantly wishing he hadn't. A wall of debris hurtles toward them at great speed, one which threatens to engulf them at any moment. Just as he is about to give up, the vehicle's track finds purchase in the soft ground, and digs in, clawing them out of harm's way with mere seconds to spare.

Suddenly a shattered tree trunk bobs out of the water, slides up the river bank, and slams into the rear of the vehicle. The girl and the woman scream as they are viciously shoved to one side and almost tossed off. The log punctures the rear cover, jamming into place. The log's far end swirls around, caught in the raging current, and drags the vehicle back into the rising waters.

In sheer desperation, Joe applies full power as he stands up and leans the machine over, tipping the damaged side down and deeper into the water. The log shifts, then lifts free of the back of the machine, to swirl away, leaving them floundering on the river's edge. The hole in the rear quickly fills with water, threatening to drag them under.

Somehow, Joe maneuvers the damaged vehicle up the slippery river bank, where he stops, well clear of any debris.

Getting off, the woman points to the damaged track and bluntly states, "We aren't going anywhere on that thing, not anymore. It's ruined!"

Joe stares at the chewed-up track which has slipped off its guide rails, then plonks heavily to the ground, defeated.

Though still shaking from the fear and cold, the girl offers a thin smile as she addresses Joe, "Thank you for saving the lady. I'm sure she is grateful."

The woman lowers her gaze, abashed by the young girl's comment, then says, "Yes. Thank you." A moment later she mumbles, "Sorry."

Joe wakes with a start; his pulse races as he looks around anxiously. His breathing comes in short, fast, bursts, as he comes to terms with what he sees. The ceiling is of his holiday suite, as is the pillow he lays on, and the bed he is in. It was all a crazy dream! He has no idea what happened after Miranda led him to his bed, nor where she is. He is alone.

He throws the blankets off, then stops. His toes are bandaged, and he is wearing pajamas. He frowns deeply; he does not own any pajamas. Sliding to the edge of the bed, his hands catch on the sheets. He stares at them, surprised. They are rough, and look as if they were exposed to cold weather for too long.

He stands up gingerly; his toes hurt, but only a little.

The door to his room opens unexpectedly, and in walks a nurse. She steps toward Joe and asks, "And how are we today?"

"Today?" Joe replies. He shakes his foggy head, then asks, "What happened?"

"Oh, nothing really, you just wandered off the resort's property and got lost, that's all." She answers as she checks his blood pressure and temperature.

Joe has no idea what she is talking about, and asks, "How long have I been here?"

"Just two days sweetheart," she replies with a smile, then says, "just in time to leave, unfortunately."

Joe is baffled. All he recalls is the avalanche and the rush of icy water, nothing which matches wandering off.

Meanwhile, in another room, Miranda turns to Gordon and says, "I told you he had no tracking devices. I performed a full bio-scan when he was in the tank, and then checked all his gear while the memory scan ran its course."

Gordon taps the table between them as he considers what to do, then says, "I smell a trap. We'll wait for next time."

She sighs as she replies, "Henry was one of our best, and they got him. I just want to know what he told Joe."

"Well, according to the regression therapy, nothing of consequence." Gordon replies.

Miranda hesitantly asks, "Why'd you injure him?"

"I want Joe to wonder if his experience was real or not. But more importantly, I want to see if any of this makes it to the authorities." Gordon replies. Smiling, he adds, "It does help having a nurse on the payroll."

She nods, then says, "The next time he comes here… there will be a next time, won't there?" she questions, interrupting her own thoughts.

"Oh yes." Gordon nods, "I'll make sure of it."

"Good," she states, then finishes her initial thought, "I have no doubt I'll be able to get his attention." Miranda chuckles as she shakes her head, adding, "He's so easy."

Gordon slowly shakes his head as he states, "You poured the charm on so thick, I thought for sure you'd scare him off."

"Charm?" she questions indignantly, putting her hands on her hips. "I work with the assets I have!" She states while lifting her eyebrows.

"Oh, you have assets darling, you have assets." Gordon mumbles wistfully.

She smiles cheekily as she gets up and leaves, ignoring his comments. Miranda knows Gordon is rich, and desires her, but she is not interested in being some rich man's play thing. She grins as she realizes that of all the men she has met in their rooms, she has slept with none. Something she intends to maintain. She pauses in her thoughts, then sighs with a twinge of sadness. But, thanks to her role, she has gained the reputation of being a busy girl. No one wants a serious relationship with her; instead she spends much of her time turning down lurid offers from people who think that is what she is like.

Later that evening, the nurse returns to Joe's suite, removes the bandages from his feet, and offers him two tubes of cream. "These are for your hands." she states, then with a smile adds, "They'll heal up in no time."

33

The morning's sunlight shines through the open drapes, rousing Joe from his slumber. He rubs his hands together, and finds to his joy that they feel much smoother. His toes have almost fully healed as well, allowing him to put his socks and shoes on relatively easily. He sighs; the nurse was correct, he will be one hundred percent tomorrow, his first day back at work. He eats breakfast, then stops as he realizes that something does not add up. Three days, and three nights, and yet the nurse had said *two days*, plus the day he arrived, and today, the day he leaves. Well, that could technically be a three-night vacation he muses, then returns to his bacon and eggs. Pausing once more, his eyes narrow as he wonders how he slept so long, especially as his injuries seem minor. There is also the matter of him having no memory of walking anywhere. The last thing he remembers seeing, is Miranda's beautiful eyes and radiant smile.

Chapter Three –Reality Check

Reluctantly, he packs his clothing, and then walks to the front desk, toting his luggage. A young man checks him out, then as he is about to leave, hands Joe an envelope.

Joe takes it as he asks, "What's this?"

The young man ignores the question, stacks a few brochures, then leaves the desk, stepping into a private area and out of sight.

Joe sighs as he puts the envelope in his pocket. He casts his gaze around the magnificent entry area once more, then steps outside to his waiting vehicle. Recalling his vivid dream, he glances toward the distant mountains, then wiggles his fingers as he stares at them. His memories conflict with what he was told happened, but then his dream is an impossibility, while wandering off drunk, is quite plausible. He gets inside his vehicle, then sits back and relaxes as he is driven back to the city.

Miranda paces back and forth behind a huge window on the top floor, while Gordon stands, staring at the retreating vehicle.

She stops pacing, then shakes her head as she states, "This is too dangerous. You risk us all!"

"I risk nothing." Gordon replies as he continues to watch Joe's vehicle travel along the road. He looks over his shoulder to her as he states, "We'll know if the Central Authority has an interest in him this way."

Joe wakes, alarmed, it is dark outside. He sits up and immediately relaxes, he is in the transit tunnel. He does not know when the tunnel was built, but he does know that the government is proud of their achievement. Rather than run roadways across the lush farmland, the road was constructed under it. He lays back and falls asleep, as he did the first time going through the tunnel.

BLEEP... BLEEP... BLEEP...

Joe shuts his alarm off, then stretches as he gets out of bed. He gazes around, perplexed. His vacation clothes are put away, while his work clothes are hanging on his rack, cleaned and pressed. He has no recollection of when he did all of this, nor when he actually arrived home. He notices the envelope given to him at the resort sits unopened, on his side dresser.

He opens it and reads the brief note, 'I hope you get to come back and see me again. – Miranda.' He smiles, and yet also feels a little at odds with himself as he wonders what her interest is in him. He sighs, then yawning, he rubs his eyes. With all the sleep he has been getting, he cannot believe he feels so tired.

He is almost late for work, but quickly gets back into his office routine. He soon forgets about the mystery of how he got to be in his bed, but the dream of the snowy mountain top stays with him, hauntingly.

Central Authority

Doctor Liang turns to Arnold and says, "Well, the interception of his vehicle was successful, and you were right. The Subverts do have an interest in him!"

"I reviewed his memory scan, just like you did, and saw nothing of the sort." Arnold replies bluntly.

"What about the false memory engram?" Liang presses, lifting his eyebrows.

"That is unusual, but then, it is a holiday resort." Arnold replies, as if his answer were the explanation.

Liang grins as he explains, "Someone scanned his memory, but unlike our current methods, they created a fantasy scenario to keep his mind occupied while they did it."

Arnold takes a deep breath, then says, "Look, it took considerable effort to intercept his vehicle in the tunnel, and load it into the transit truck for your examination. I do not see how we really gained anything worthwhile."

Liang's grin widens as he replies, "We know someone scanned his memory, and other than us, the only people who do that, are Subverts."

Arnold considers how he can report this positively, and yet still be immune from any failure of their plan. After a moment, he asks, "Your recommendations?"

Doctor Liang replies quickly, "Send him back to the resort." He narrows his eyes as he adds, "We did conduct a low-level memory wipe."

"Low level?" Arnold questions, then states, "But, if his mind is scanned, recollections of our memory scans may surface."

Excitement almost overcomes Liang as he replies, "Exactly!"

"But Joe will not have any memory of this." Arnold states, then as he realizes what the Doctor intends, adds, "which will baffle the Subverts as Joe is clearly not an agent of ours."

Doctor Liang taps his fingers on his desk as he says, "I have no idea what they will do next. They will know that he knows nothing, and that we know this too."

Arnold stares at Liang as he replies, "If they're smart, they'll leave him alone, but then again…" his voice trails off.

"Joe has become an unwitting pawn in our game of cat and mouse." Liang comments, stating the obvious.

"Indeed!" Arnold replies.

Liang maintains a stoic expression, concealing his excitement at the prospect of learning more about the Subverts. He is also perplexed as to why his supervisors have provided him with access to more and more archived data, and how it could possibly relate to his current mission. He plans to review these archives, to learn all he can.

Chapter Four – Resort Revisited

Joe works hard each day, and dreams of Miranda at night. Hoping to earn another visit to the resort, he spends more time at work than he used to, researching and learning, and finds that he is gaining a fresh insight into the stock market. He notices trends and fluctuations that seem to defy expected market tendencies, and capitalizes on his discoveries, increasing the wealth of his clients. He reviews his company's policies, and the law governing self-investment, and finds to his surprise that it is relatively easy to start his own portfolio, which he does in earnest with his meager savings. It does not take him long to boost his own worth, all legally.

"Joe!" A voice calls out urgently.

Joe lifts his head sharply, then grins when he sees Gordon. He strides to the man and smiles as he shakes his hand. Others in the office stare, stupefied, none of them dare be as familiar with, 'the Legend'.

"Any advice for me Joe?" Gordon asks, soliciting a mixture of snickers and snorts from those around him.

Joe lowers his gaze, he knows that Gordon is making fun of him.

"I'm serious." Gordon states, then turns to the others, venomously adding, "Joe has increased the value of his clients' portfolios by eighteen percent!"

"That's not so much." A voice calls out from the back of the office, "Many of us achieved fifteen percent gains this year."

Gordon stares in the direction of the voice, and then loudly states, "This quarter!"

Joe's eyes flicker; it dawns on him that Gordon is serious, and not making fun of him at all. He lifts his gaze and smiles once more. He has been so busy, he had not even looked at how well he was doing compared to others in the company.

Gordon turns to Joe and says, "Listen, I just spoke to the board, and convinced them that you need a real vacation, especially since the last one was spoiled."

Joe is floored, "You spoke to the board, about me?"

"Yes." Gordon replies matter-of-factly, then adds, "You work hard, and deserve the rewards that go with success."

"When do you think I'll be able to go?" Joe asks, secretly hoping it is sooner than later.

"Well," Gordon replies slowly, "how about we get a workstation installed in your suite, and then you could stay for two weeks?"

"WOW!" Joe exclaims, stunned by the idea of working from the resort.

There is silence in the office as those around realize that instead of shunning the newcomer, Joe, they should have worked with him. He has eclipsed all of them, and he has done so in a short amount of time.

Gordon smiles widely as he says, "I take it that's a yes, in which case, I will see you at the resort in two days."

"Two days," Joe replies softly, still trying to come to terms with the whole vacation plan. His wildest dreams are coming true, and far sooner than even he dared imagine.

The two days seem to drag on as Joe continues to work diligently. Finally, the end of the second day arrives. He gazes around the office, then realizing he is alone, shuts his terminal down, and leaves. He should be tired, but instead has an energetic spring to his step.

Joe is wide awake this trip, and although he keeps looking for the mountains, they do not come into view until his vehicle exits the long tunnel. The moment he sees them, he feels relieved, as though he were home. He is still confused as to how he can recall the dream of them so well, and yet not a thing about wandering off and getting frostbite. He puts it all out of his mind as he relaxes.

Exiting his vehicle, he hurries inside, and is immediately disappointed. A young man stands behind the desk, and not Miranda as he had hoped. He is surprised when he is assigned the same suite, and even more so to find a computer terminal on the small table with the exquisite light. He checks the terminal, and finds that it is wired into the wall, to sockets which look as though they have always been there.

Although fully dressed, Joe lays on the bed and puts his hands behind his head. He takes a deep breath, taking in the freshness of the room, and smiles. He closes his eyes as he relaxes and enjoys his surroundings. He falls into a deep asleep almost immediately.

Sunken City

Joe opens his eyes and looks around nervously. He is standing on a hot, sandy plain; a warm breeze blows in his face, bringing with it fine grains which sting his skin. He squints through the haze at a cluster of thirty or so tall buildings. They are within walking distance but appear to have been abandoned long ago, judging by their broken windows and crumbling facades. Looking around, sparse hills block his view, leaving the city as the only thing of interest. Some of the buildings reach forty stories high, others are shorter, with the smallest being twenty-three stories.

A low rumbling beneath his feet alerts him to the earthquake before it hits. He staggers as the sand around him dances with the vibrations. Inexplicably, one of the buildings begins to sink, followed by another, then another. Soon, all of them are sliding beneath the ground.

The shortest building disappears completely, leaving a rough divot in its wake. The rumbling and shaking stops, as does the descent of the buildings, leaving the tallest of them with only their upper levels exposed. A low dust cloud hangs over the buildings, the only sign that anything odd has just occurred.

A young girl's shrill scream pierces the air, echoing up and down the valley.

Joe spins to face the source, then rushes toward one of the buildings, his arms and legs pumping like pistons as he sprints forward. More than half of the building has been completely consumed, leaving the rest sticking upward; jagged tops and spires rising above the swirling sands. He

dashes through the shattered remnants of a
window, and comes crashing down in a corridor.
Still sprinting, he bolts for a stairwell, and rushes
downward. At each level, he can see where the
outer portions of the building have been breached
by sand.

A voice calls out from far below, the words
unintelligible, but the fear in them is a palpable
thing. Joe is alarmed to see the bottom of the
stairwell filling. He does not question how he can
see; there is no visible light source, yet he is able to
discern many details, like the flaking paint on the
handrail which descends into the bowels of the
building.

"I'm coming!" Joe hears himself shout, as
though he were undergoing an out of body
experience.

"Here! In here!" Calls the young voice
frantically.

Sand is filling the shaft, having already
engulfed the lower levels. Joe dives out of the
stairwell, and into a silt filled office area. A young
girl rushes to him, then jumps on him; the same
one he rescued from the icy avalanche.

"You came for me." She sobs through tear
filled eyes, her long brown hair dust filled and
matted.

"I did." Joe responds, then quickly states, "We
must hurry!"

"Did you find the lady?" The girl questions, her
face scrunched in a worried frown.

"Lady?" Joe questions as the girl lets her feet
slide to the floor, and take her own weight.

"Help…" A feeble voice calls from somewhere
nearby.

Joe looks around, but is unable to see anyone. Sand is slowly spilling in through the broken windows, and will soon engulf the entire level. Looking back at the stairwell he can see more falling from above in ever increasing cascades.

"I'm trapped!" the feeble voice calls out, "I can't get out."

Joe spins around to face the direction of the voice, and while holding the girl's hand, rushes past desks and partitions, searching. He finds her, laying on the ground, her legs trapped beneath a large cabinet. Sand spills in from a missing window; it already covers her feet and will soon engulf her.

"Are you hurt?" Joe asks, concerned.

"No, just stuck." The lady replies, dread building in her voice as she tries to pull herself out. Her lips quiver as tears spill down her face.

Joe lifts the corner of the cabinet with all his might, lifting it just enough for her to slide out. She rubs her lower legs; they are scratched and bruised, but other than that, she seems uninjured.

The lady hobbles as she leans on Joe, hurrying as best she can. Joe puts his arm around her ample waist as he tries to support some of her weight.

The girl rushes ahead and makes it to the stairwell first. As she pushes her way through the deepening sand, she shouts anxiously, "Hurry up. It's filling!"

Joe and the lady arrive at the stairwell where they wade through the knee-deep sand; the lower levels are completely buried. More cascades from above, covering them in fine dust as the three of them climb the stairs. They continue upward until they see sunlight filtering in, casting a hazy glow everywhere. The girl motions frantically for them to hurry as she stares outside, to freedom.

Joe helps the lady out through an opening, then as a renewed rumbling vibrates through the ground, he lunges out, and escapes the building.

The dust covered trio staggers on the moving sands, then once they are well clear of the buildings, Joe flops to the ground, exhausted.

"Look!" The girl shouts as she points to the buildings.

Joe watches as the ground swallows the tallest of them, leaving virtually no sign they existed at all. He closes his eyes while he catches his breath.

The woman sits on the ground next to him and says, "Thank you again."

Joe's eyes fling open as he repeats, "Again?"

Staring at the ceiling of his suite, he is baffled. Standing, he discovers that once again, he is wearing pajamas. Walking to the drapes, he flings them open. The sun is rising in the distance, casting shadows on the dew-covered grass.

He goes to the bathroom, then as he washes his hands he pauses. They are dry and rough.

Gordon stares at Miranda as he states, "The Central Authority knows someone here scanned his memory, and now they'll learn we've just done it again." He shakes his head, then says, "I'm so stupid. We may have just as well advertised that we're here at the resort!"

Miranda sighs, "It's ironic that a man who knows nothing about us, could indeed lead to our downfall."

"We have too much at stake to let them scan his mind again." Gordon states, "But…" He adds as an idea forms.

"But... what?" Miranda questions, wondering what he has in mind.

"What if Joe were to disappear?" Gordon asks, "And I mean really disappear."

"Subvert him?" Miranda questions, "But he knows nothing." She presses.

"We'll show him." Gordon replies, "And then let him decide what he wants to do."

Miranda stares hard at Gordon, then says, "You're right. If we send him back the authorities will know for sure that this resort is a front, or at the very least being used by us."

"Exactly!" Gordon replies, "But, if we send him back, after his vacation, and intercept him in the tunnel, before they do, hopefully the authorities will think that is where we, or I should say *they*, are operating."

Chapter Five – Truth Revealed

Arnold reads the report and flinches. Turning to Liang he questions, "Gone?"

Nervous and hot, Doctor Liang pulls at his shirt collar. He swallows hard as he replies, "Yes. We monitored his vehicle entering the tunnel, and have surveillance images showing he was in the vehicle at the time. But when the extraction team went to retrieve him, he was gone."

Arnold stomps, pacing back and forth angrily as he considers what will happen to him with this failure. It dawns on him that he has not failed, he has succeeded. With a wolfish grin, he orders, "We'll search the tunnel's subsystems for Subverts. They must have a base of operations nearby."

"And the resort?" Liang asks.

"We'll raid it later. Let them think they're safe, for now!"

Liang nods to Arnold, then says, "My superiors will want to know what has happened. I will report this personally." He is not sure what will happen to him, he had, after all, followed his directives to the letter.

Joe feels groggy and sluggish as he wakes. His vacation was amazing, and even though he is returning to work, he is already looking forward to his next trip.

He opens his eyes, then jumps. His breaths become quick and short as he looks around, alarmed. He is laying on a rough bunk, in a white room. Bright lights glare down on him.

Gordon walks over and says, "I have some things I think you need to see."

Joe frowns as he replies, "Me?"

"Yes, you!"

Joe's heart races as he sits up. He fearfully asks, "Where am I?"

"Safe." Gordon replies, then with a sigh, adds, "You were being used by the Central Authority."

"I don't understand." Joe replies meekly, looking around the bare room.

Gordon takes a deep breath as he considers how to summarize everything, then begins. "Henry was one of our top members. When he approached you, he started a chain of events. Both us, and the Central Authority, wanted to find out what he told you."

Joe frowns in confusion, "He didn't say anything special, just something about fixers and machines. I think."

"We know that now!" Gordon replies as he paces back and forth. He stops, then staring at Joe, adds, "But, in the process of us learning that, the authorities gained proof that we were operating out of the resort."

Joe lowers his gaze as he mumbles, "That's why Miranda was flirting with me."

"That's her roll in our organization."

"So those crazy dreams?" Joe questions.

Gordon nods as he replies, "That's how we scan a person's memories, by planting a dream which keeps the person's mind focused."

Joe frowns as he presses, "So the girl and woman I rescued are all just part of the dream you created?"

"Girl, woman?" Gordon repeats, confused. "What girl and woman?" He demands, curiosity mounting.

Joe glances around nervously as he answers, "In both dreams I was with a young girl, and we rescued a woman."

Gordon glances to one of the walls, then says, "That's something for our people to figure out."

Joe stands up, feeling dizzy, he holds onto the table. He slowly shakes his head as he asks, "So what'll happen now? I guess I'm not going back to work."

Gordon chuckles, "No, you're not going back to work. As for what happens next, well, I want to show you the world you live in. The real world."

Joe is confused, and a little afraid. But he has come to like Gordon, and does not feel the man would do anything to harm him.

Canfield Airport

Dozens of people are milling about; some are seated, while others walk aimlessly around as they wait for flights. The city's airport terminal has many small lounges, each with a grand view of the runways, planes, and buildings. An auto-cop stands near a wall, diligently monitoring everything.

Gordon stands, stretches, then tells Joe, "Follow me."

Joe nods as he walks toward a huge window, through which they can see the airport. The tarmac below shimmers in the sunlight, while the concrete runways stretch off to the left and right. A large passenger plane is parked, connected to an out of sight airport lounge by a jetway. A small yellow vehicle pulls a convoy of carts, each loaded with luggage.

Joe smiles, he has never travelled by plane, but one day hopes to.

"Okay," Gordon states, a seriousness entering his tone, "as I told you before, I can turn off the signals to your ocular implants."

"I still have trouble believing everything you've told me." Joe replies.

Gordon smiles as he looks around, then instructs, "It is imperative that you do not react, no matter what you see, do not change your facial expression, and do not move. Is that understood?"

"Yes," Joe replies, then asks, "but if this is so dangerous to you, why am I here?"

Gordon sighs, then says, "It's important that you see the world for what it is."

"Well, I'm ready." Joe replies, still doubting all that Gordon has told him.

Gordon reaches into his pocket, and then after a brief hesitation, presses a button on the small device he carries.

Joe feels a chill run up his spine as the scene outside instantly changes. He gulps as he tries to remain calm. The jetway is in tatters, with sections of canvas blowing in the wind. The concrete runways are full of craters, with grass and shrubs growing from vast cracks. Off in the distance, a massive concrete wall rises into the sky. The biggest shock though, is the plane. It is rusted, with one wing broken, and though still partially connected to the fuselage, its tip rests on the tarmac. Dirt and debris hang out of its ruined engines, while nearby, the small yellow vehicle and its carts, rests, rusted and abandoned. He looks back at the airport lounge, and finds it looks almost exactly the same, as does the auto-cop which stands where it did before.

Gordon clicks the hidden device again as he instructs, "Just follow me, and smile. I can answer all your questions in a little while."

Joe turns to look outside again. He watches as the pristine looking yellow vehicle parks near the plane, and two people begin transferring luggage from the carts to the planes hold. He then turns and follows Gordon, stunned. His heart starts beating faster as his mind tries to rationalize what he just witnessed.

A few moments later, Gordon says, "You coped with that quite well. Perhaps I should show you more."

"More?" Joe questions, "What more can there be?"

"A lot more!"

Joe frowns, then says, "But I know people who have flown!"

"Do you?" Gordon replies, then stopping he turns and says, "They travelled on trains to their destinations."

"Trains!" Joe exclaims a little too loudly.

"Think about it." He presses, "The inside of a plane is simply a long tube."

"What about turbulence?" Joe questions with a frown.

"We have rides at the theme park which simulate flight, and turbulence, with great realism from what I hear. Consider that." Gordon states as he lifts his eyebrows.

"But why would they do this?" Joe asks, becoming concerned.

"This is how they keep the population content, and oblivious to reality."

A family of five rushes by, interrupting their debate. The father is carrying two large suitcases, and telling them to hurry up or they will miss their flight. The mother holds the hands of two young children, while the remaining child, a teenager, is also carrying a pair of suitcases.

As casually as possible Joe glances to Gordon, and smiles thinly.

Gordon notices Joe's face is splotchy, with his pulse visibly throbbing in his neck. He knows they must get out of there, now!

Once the family has moved past, Gordon states, "Our lives are a farce. Yes, we work where we work, sleep where we sleep, but as for the rest, there is so much more."

"But what of all the money I manage for people?" Joe asks, numbed.

"It's just a game to them."

"But some people are rich and powerful!"

"Are they?" Gordon questions, "Or are we led to believe they are because of a few numbers on a computer screen?"

"But the powerful people run the city." Joe states, not giving up on his thinking.

"They think they do!" Gordon states, then says, "They live in larger homes, own a few more toys, but at the end of the day, they're no different to you or me."

Joe gazes around, stunned, then requests, "Can we go past where I lived?"

"That would be too dangerous, sector one is crawling with auto-cops." Gordon replies as he gazes around apprehensively.

"No, I mean my old place." Joe pleads.

Gordon grinds his jaw as he considers the risks, then says, "We can travel down the street, but we won't stop."

"Can you turn this thing off while we do? I want to see where I was really living."

"Of course, now get in." Gordon instructs as he motions to his vehicle.

The journey to Joe's old street does not take long. Once there, Gordon shuts off the data feed to Joe's implants. He feels sad for Joe as he watches the man's life he knew being stripped away. He knows the feelings all too well, he was the same when he learned the truth.

Joe looks for the area where he tripped and shakes his head when he sees that the pavement is chipped and broken. The huge screen on the nearby wall is simply a dirty canvas. He is surprised to see that the grass and shrubs are real, however they look sickly. The buildings are in good shape, while the road itself is surprisingly okay.

Gordon watches Joe's numbed expression, and explains, "Things that people interact with, such as walkways, roads, trees, and pretty much anything in reach, must be maintained to keep the illusion alive. But other than that, things like that wall-viewer, well they're out of reach, and can be augmented."

Joe glances up as they pass a set of traffic lights, they appear dead, yet Joe has stood at the corner, and waited for the walk signal many times. Joe meekly asks, "The park. Can I see it?"

Gordon replies solemnly, "You don't want to. The trees are real, as is the water in the fountain, but there are no animals." He lowers his head as he adds, "We don't even know if there are any real animals left."

Joe gazes at the real world, stunned, as they continue. Almost everything is run down and dilapidated, surprisingly though, a few of the streets and buildings are in good condition, and obviously maintained.

Gordon glances to Joe, then shares, "What we do know, is that the world ran out of resources, and while some countries, like ours, took desperate measures to preserve the little that was left, others went to war."

Joe frowns, confused, then questions, "War? I don't see any signs of war."

"Oh, you will soon enough." Gordon states, then solemnly repeats, "You will soon enough."

They drive away from the city, and their homes. Gordon sighs inwardly as they travel further, he too is leaving everything behind. He hopes that Miranda has been successful, otherwise they will eventually end up in the hands of the Central Authority.

The Wall

Joe's eyes widen as they approach a massive wall which curves high into the sky. He blinks and shakes his head; he is looking at the impossible..

As the vehicle stops, Gordon states, "We must hurry, before the authorities get here."

Joe steps out and gazes upward at the curved wall. He is unable to see where it ends, and the sky begins.

"Gentlemen, hurry!" Miranda calls out, an urgency in her tone.

Joe spins around, surprised by the sound of her voice. She is standing in a doorway in the wall, wearing rough pants along with a thick shirt. Not exactly as attractive as the last outfit he saw her in.

"HURRY!" She screeches loudly as she looks around frantically.

Gordon tosses two small objects into the vehicle as he instructs, "Home." He then takes off running toward Miranda, while Joe remains where he is, baffled. There is no threat. Then, as the vehicle leaves, he hears something; a low humming sound, and it is getting louder. He sprints after Gordon.

Joe rushes through the doorway, which Miranda slams shut behind him. She glances at Gordon and says, "This had better be worth it. We've both lost our covers, and our dome."

"Yes, we've lost our homes." Joe replies gloomily, thinking that is what she said.

"Dome, not home," She corrects.

"Dome!" Joe repeats loudly, his jaw dropping. "I was living in a dome," the realization just hitting him.

"Yes," Gordon replies.

Miranda ignores the men as she receives instructions through her small earpiece. "Yes!" she shouts excitedly, punching the air. With a wide grin, she relays, "There's a vehicle waiting for us in bay seven."

Joe glances around, then looks upward. They are standing between two curved walls, connected above by a vast array of interlocking metal beams which stretch off into the distance, and out of sight. Lights line the slightly curved walkway in both directions; some flicker irregularly, whilst others are not working at all. He takes a deep breath, then scrunches up his nose; the air is stale and musty. Listening carefully, an occasional drip pings off metal somewhere, yet there are no pools of water to indicate where the drops are landing.

"This way." Gordon says, as he relaxes; he had not known if they would receive any assistance and is relieved to learn that their plea for help has been answered.

Gordon does not delay and leads them along the wide corridor at a brisk pace. They hurry past an area which has a massive faded number two on the wall. The next number is quite a distance away, and as they approach can see it is an equally faded, number three.

Joe glances back fearfully, then asks, "Aren't you afraid they'll follow us?"

Miranda smiles as she replies, "Your bio trackers were destroyed earlier, while ours are in the vehicle. It should take them a while to figure out where we are, and by the time they do, we'll be long gone."

Gordon recalls the debate he had with Miranda, and how she convinced him to get his removed. It was an uncomfortable process; they had to remain functional, as if still in his body, thus small chunks of living tissue were taken with each one. Then, they were sealed inside a small bio-canister, which Gordon carried at all times to maintain his cover, another illusion. Joe was the lucky one, his were surgically removed and destroyed when they took him in the tunnel and put him to sleep. Miranda's had also been taken out, a while ago, and given to Gordon for safe keeping. The only remaining concern is the ocular implants; they are fully grafted to their eyes and can only be deactivated, not removed.

"Careful." Gordon states as he focuses on the present, almost walking into a pile of rusty beams.

Joe stares wide-eyed at the beams, and the deep gouges in the concrete where they struck when they fell. Water trickles down the walls, forming pools in which grows a strange green velvety substance. He has never seen moss before and does not know what it is. Peering upward into the darkness, he is unable to see where the water is coming from. He sniffs warily at an odd, unpleasant odor which wafts in the air. He quickly glances at Miranda and Gordon, but they seem unconcerned with the smell.

Miranda notices Joe's inquisitiveness, and says, "The outer dome cracked long ago, damage I would expect to have been repaired immediately." She sighs as she adds, "But it would seem that the Central Authority has given up on maintaining the outer dome all together."

Gordon nods as he adds his thoughts, "The bright side is that there are no repair crews, or anything else, to stop us."

Joe's jaw drops as he says, "So, anyone could just walk in here from outside?"

"Ah, not exactly." Gordon hesitantly replies, then adds, "You'll see."

They eventually arrive at bay seven, where a small bus-like vehicle with four large bulbous tires is waiting. Joe follows Gordon and Miranda inside, and is surprised when the pair nods to another person who is waiting for them. The vehicle has seats for six passengers, along with the driver. The forward section has a wide curved window, while each of the passenger seats has a smaller window.

The man nods back as he states, "It took you long enough!"

Gordon grins as he replies, "It's good to see you too, Pete."

Pete motions to Joe and asks, "So, is this the one?"

"Yes," Gordon replies.

"What do you mean, 'The one?'" Joe asks, confused by the question.

Miranda turns to Joe as she replies, "The reason our cover was blown with the Central Authority."

"Oh." Joe replies sullenly. "It wasn't my fault." He mumbles.

Pete flicks a series of switches on his console as he instructs, "Let's get out of here. We can talk later."

A deep rumbling emanates through the floor as a large section of the outer wall lifts. A hazy blue-green mist ominously wafts in. As soon as there is enough room for the vehicle, Pete drives through the opening, and outside. Once clear of the dome, he flicks a switch back, closing the entryway.

Visibility is not as bad as Joe had expected, and yet is still limited to less than a city block. A mist hugs the ground, hiding it from view, thinning as it gets higher in the air. The sun's rays filter through the haze, revealing a bleak landscape. Grey dust forms a cloud in their wake as they travel over the rough ground. The vehicle's flexible suspension system allows the wheels to track across the bumps and hollows of the land with ease, keeping them relatively level. The deeper divots cause them to tilt, and some bumps jostle them in their seats, yet the ride is surprisingly comfortable.

"What happened?" Joe asks.

Gordon motions outside as he replies, "I told you earlier that the world ran out of resources, and some countries went to war. Well, this is the result!"

Pete grimaces as he swerves around a crater he had forgotten about. Without taking his eyes off the way ahead, he states, "According to the old calendar, the wars started over four hundred years ago, with the oldest domes pre-dating that time."

Joe frowns in confusion as he asks, "But if resources were running out that long ago, how is it we still have stuff?"

Pete sighs, then replies, "To the best of my knowledge, our planet's population peaked at twenty-three billion, while today, we estimate there to be some quarter-million survivors." He glances to Joe as he further explains, "Your community is one of the smaller groups, with the largest having around a hundred thousand people."

Joe's jaw drops disbelievingly as he states, "Canfield has over a million people!"

Gordon leans over and puts a hand on Joe's arm, comforting him as he replies, "No. Our dome has a population of thirty-six thousand, four hundred and ninety, give or take a few."

Miranda looks across with sorrowful eyes as she adds, "The Central Authority is trying to perpetuate our old way of life, but even they have to realize the truth."

She gazes outside for a few moments then murmurs, "Most women are sterile; the world's population is declining."

Joe follows her gaze, then excitedly points as he blurts, "What's that?" A tall, eroded structure looms out of the mist. It is connected to their dome by a pitted and crumbling passageway.

Pete swivels his head around, alarmed, then heaves a sigh of relief when he sees what Joe is referring to. They are all on edge, and Joe's tone got their pulses racing. He focuses on the terrain ahead, choosing the best route possible through the misty landscape.

As the structure fades into the mist, Joe looks at Gordon and asks once more, "What was that building?"

"The water purification plant." Gordon replies, "It ceased being used when the ocean became too toxic."

Pete glances back as he hears the explanation but says nothing.

Miranda stares out the window as she states, "Pete, take us via the coastal route, Joe should see it for himself."

"Okay, will do." Pete replies, concentrating hard on his task.

Climbing a small hill, they rise above the mist, allowing them a grand view of the surrounding landscape. Joe stares back at the dome, its bulk rises out of the haze and high into the sky, like the monolith it is. He squints at a discolored section in the dome's top, then notices other areas which are crumbling away. The tall structure he saw earlier comes into view once more, as do tops of other distant domes. He resists the urge to ask more questions, instead, he takes in the scene, letting the ramifications of what he is learning sink in.

Traveling down the far side of the hill, they reenter the mist once more, subduing them all. They remain quiet as they continue onward. Occasionally they climb other small hills, lifting them out of the murk over and over. Each time they clear the fog, Joe glances back at the dome which was his home, until they are too far away to discern it through the haze.

Joe desperately wants to ask dozens of questions, but he can feel the tension in the air, and waits. Glancing upward to the hazy sun, it dawns on him that he has no idea which direction they are going. He then realizes that is does not matter.

The Ocean

Pete glances at his controls, then stops the vehicle as he states, "We've made it to the coast road."

"Road!" Joe exclaims, surprised.

Pete grins as he replies, "Yes. We maintain some of the roads, as best we can anyway."

Miranda interrupts any more questions when she says, "Joe, we'll explain everything later on." She turns to Pete and asks, "Is the high road safe?"

Pete nods as he replies, "We haven't seen any drones for a while." He shrugs, "It should be."

Gordon nods as he says, "I agree with Miranda, it's the shortest route."

They do not travel long before they climb out of the haze, and this time they stay above it. The high road hugs a cliff edge and offers a panoramic view of the landscape.

Joe is stunned by the sight. Snow covered mountains line the horizon on one side, while the other reveals a vast undulating ocean of soupy rubbish. A thin fog hovers over the floating garbage for far as he can see. Trash filled waves roll onto the debris filled beach, then as the water recedes, some of the refuse is dragged back into the water, to repeat the process, over and over.

Miranda notices Joe's expression, and points to the ocean, saying, "The air is most deadly there, whereas inland, people have been known to survive outside for up to fifteen minutes."

Joe gulps, then asks, "Where'd all that rubbish come from?"

"The oceans rose, flooding cities, plus some of the early domes simply dumped their effluent into them." She replies. Turning to face Joe, she states, "You're looking at the legacy of what happens when billions of people die, leaving no one left to clean up the mess."

Pete taps his windscreen as he says, "In the early days the atmosphere was so corrosive, these babies only lasted one trip, maybe two. Luckily, we were able to manufacture acid resistant seals, windows, wheels, and just about everything else, before the vehicle plants shut down fully. Nowadays, we scrounge around to keep as many of these babies running as we can."

Gordon gazes at the rubbish covered ocean and asks, "Has anyone heard from Aqua?"

Pete shakes his head, "There was a massive earthquake a while back." He looks at Gordon as he adds sorrowfully, "We've heard nothing since."

Joe stares at the water blankly as he undertones, "Underwater domes!"

Gordon replies, "They were the most successful, at first. But no one expected we'd have to live in them for so long. The designers expected the protective domes would be needed for two hundred years, max." Well, it's been nearly double that, and still nothing can live outside, not yet anyway."

A fleeting memory enters Joe's mind. He looks at the mountains and comments, "They look like the mountains I could see from the resort."

"They are!" Gordon replies, happy for the change of topic. He grins as he adds, "But these are the real ones."

Joe recalls his vivid dream of the mountain, then recalls Gordon's admission that it was all a planted memory. He wonders what the woman and girl have to do with it all, as even Gordon seemed surprised when he mentioned the pair. He keeps his thoughts to himself, for now.

Central Authority

Doctor Liang stares at the canister, bewildered. His face spasms nervously at the ramifications of what he holds. *People not being where we think they are.* The thought comes unbidden, and with it, apprehension. He had not expected them to leave the dome, but then, the more he learns from the archives, the more he is beginning to understand the greater world. He wonders what his superiors will make of this development, then, in a flash of insight it dawns on him that this is possibly what they wanted.

Arnold takes a deep breath, then interrupts the doctor's thoughts, "I have ordered a recovery effort, and sent a retrieval team outside."

Liang turns and says, "Just let them go. The resources required for such an undertaking, far exceed any possible gains."

Arnold nods slowly as he replies, "Possibly. But, they went outside, and I for one want to know where they went."

Doctor Liang's face ticks as he debates sharing what he has recently learned. Then, as a drop of sweat works its way down his face, he says, "There are many domes, and I don't just mean ours. We have five domes which make up our *country*, and I know for a fact that ours is a small community, compared to some."

Arnold frowns as he asks, "How is it that you know of this, and I don't?"

Liang takes a deep breath, then says, "We're unable to sustain ourselves, and have been seeking help from other communities for quite some time, many years in fact."

"You're telling me that the medical branch has been secretly negotiating with outsiders!" Arnold states, aghast as he steps backward.

Liang snorts as he shakes his head, "If it were not for the efforts made generations ago, we'd all be dead by now."

"A lie!" Arnold states bluntly, putting his hands on his hips defiantly.

"Our water purification facilities stopped functioning before you were born!" Liang announces. He boldly points at Arnold, as he states, "And it's not just the water systems. Everything is at failure point."

"The auto-fixers." Arnold states, as if that were the answer to everything.

Doctor Liang shakes his head as he explains, "We replaced the people with machines so that we could perpetuate our lie a little longer." He shakes his head as he laments, "Lies within lies; we tell the people one thing, your bureau another, while head medical are the only ones who know the truth. The real truth."

"What is that truth then?" Arnold demands.

"I already told you." Liang replies, "Our dome is failing, and we're all dead if we don't get help, soon!"

Arnold's mind races as he considers what all this means, then with an increasing feeling of dread, says, "You wanted them to escape, to contact others." The hair raises on the back of his neck as he adds, "You people actually think the Subverts may help us."

"They may." Liang replies with a nod, then adds, "We're on the brink of extinction. They have to help, or we're all doomed."

Liang reflects on the latest report from his superiors, which has unnerved him greatly; an immediate implementation of water rationing, without explanation, unless you consider the obvious cover story given to the public of a harmful bacteria discovered in the dam. He stares at Arnold and wonders if the man even knows that there is no dam.

Arnold feels warm and uncomfortable. It never dawned on him that perhaps it was not just the general population who were being deceived. He walks to a console, then instructs the recovery team to return. They had just cleared the dome and were following tracks left by a larger vehicle.

Looking at Doctor Liang, Arnold asks, "Did it ever occur to you to ask us for help?"

Liang chuckles, "The Central Authority, helping! Now that's funny."

Arnold rubs his chin as he wonders how many others know the truth, especially considering that his request for a drone surveillance unit was denied. He glances to Liang, then frowns; he can tell the man is keeping something else from him, but is not sure what that could be.

Chapter Six – Subverts

Pete continues driving them along the coastal road for quite some time. So long that Joe begins to fidget in his seat, regretting that he did not go to the bathroom before he left. He desperately wants to ask when they will arrive at their destination, but instead waits patiently.

"DRONE!" Pete shouts as he swerves off the road, heading down into the mist between two dusty dunes. He slams on the brakes as he states, "Going passive."

Joe stares around in alarm, then swallows hard when he sees that even Gordon and Miranda are afraid.

Pete shuts the engine off, hurriedly flicks a series of switches on the console, and then waits. His fingers remain poised over the controls, ready to react if they are discovered.

"Relax, it's us." Emanates a feminine voice from the vehicle's speakers.

Pete stabs at a button as he growls, "You could've warned me! I almost messed my pants."

"I just wanted to see if my best driver had lost his edge, or not!" Replies the voice with a soft chuckle.

Pete shakes his head as he restarts the vehicle and gets them back onto the road. The terrain around them becomes rougher. The soft hills soon give way to jagged rock peaks that ominously stab upward. The road runs straight toward a massive cliff face, in which a long tunnel looms, its far side obscured by mist.

Pete takes them inside, then slows the vehicle as he explains, "There used to be orbital satellites that could track anything, but not anymore. So, we're safe."

They slow to a crawl, and then enter a side chamber. A series of massive guns line the walls. Each is recessed into the mountain, with only their barrels showing, pointing at them as they delve deeper into the mountain.

Joe glances to Gordon and Miranda. Upon seeing their numbed expressions, he asks, "Haven't you guys been here before?"

Gordon shakes his head as Miranda replies, "Our role was to simply provide a safe gateway between the outside, and the dome. The resort was perfect, as most of the wealthy are allowed special privileges, and privacy, which allowed us to arrange meetings, with relative impunity." She reflects on the one time she saw the coastal road, and the rubbish filled ocean, and does not relish the idea of being outside again.

Joe frowns as he asks, "But you two seemed especially interested in me?"

"We were." She replies, her thoughts brought back to the present, adding, "We wanted to know what Henry told you, plus we were concerned you were an agent."

"An agent?" Joe questions.

Gordon turns and looks at Joe as he says, "The Central Authority thinks the Subverts are a small group of rebellious people *inside* the dome, who interact with what they call, outsiders." He glances to Pete, then stops talking.

Joe looks from Pete to Gordon then, when no one talks, he gazes out the window once more. The closeness of the rock wall startles him, as does the speed at which they are moving. He shifts nervously away from the window as they continue.

69

Without any warning, they enter a vast underground chamber; dim lights reveal dozens of vehicles along with hundreds of people. A contingent of thirty, heavily armed guards, encircles a prominent figure, a tall, regally dressed, woman. She looks as though she belongs in a different era, or place.

Pete is the only one not awed by the chamber as he stops their vehicle. He grins as he states proudly, "Welcome to Golem One!"

The three passengers follow Pete's lead as he steps out of the vehicle, walks to the guards, and then stops.

The lady motions as she orders, "Scan them!"

Nine men carrying bulky weapons step forward, almost in unison, with three each approaching Gordon, Miranda, and Joe.

"Lift your arms." Orders the one in front of Joe, motioning with his weapon for effect.

Joe quivers in fear, his eyes locked on the waving gun, as he complies. He studies the weapon as those on either side both pat him down and scan him with devices he barely acknowledges. The triple barreled weapon is shiny. Its upper barrel is the longest, and designed for a heavy, long distance round. It could be confused for being a sniper rifle if not for the side slung grenade launcher, alongside the third barrel which houses smoke grenades. The weapon has built in scanners, as well as a mini electromagnet pulse modulator. However, Joe only knows that three barrels wave his way from time to time.

"He's clean." The man before Joe announces once he is done.

The guards inspecting Gordon and Miranda nod, then all nine return to the others, and wait.

Joe's eyes have adjusted to the dim surroundings. Lining the cave walls are hundreds, if not thousands, of windows, while high overhead, a vast network of pipes crisscrosses the ceiling.

The well-dressed lady strides forward, and says, "My name is Dianne, and I welcome you to our home." She nods to Gordon, adding, "It is a pleasure to finally meet you in person."

Gordon is stunned; all this time, she has been his outside contact. He nods as he replies, "It's good to finally meet you too."

Joe turns his attention to the regal woman and freezes. After a brief pause he hesitantly says, "I've seen you before. But in my dreams, you were overweight."

Dianne chuckles as she replies, "I doubt you'll find any overweight people here."

Joe frowns, then presses, "There was a girl as well. She was about ten years old with long, brown, hair, and this tall." He adds lifting his hand.

A guard gasps, then quickly gathers his composure.

Gordon and Miranda glance at each other, then Gordon says confidently, "We were going to report this anomaly with the scanning program."

Dianne stares at Joe, measuring him, then with a smile, replies, "No need, I added the elements myself." While staring at Joe, she adds, "They allowed Joe to react how he wanted to, providing us an insight into his psychology."

Joe lifts an eyebrow as he brazenly asks, "And what did it tell you about me?"

"This!" Dianne replies as she turns her back to Joe, "You would risk your life for me, and my daughter, which means I can trust you."

Two of the guards automatically begin to swing their weapons up, but, lower them when Dianne smiles and motions with her hand.

Joe's jaw drops as he mutters, "That was you and your daughter!"

Gordon stares at the armed men, then recalling the heavy guns they passed, asks, "Why all the hardware?"

Dianne frowns, as if confused, then slowly shakes her head as she states, "You don't know, do you?"

"Know…?" Gordon replies, his word hanging in the air.

"We're still at war." Dianne replies.

"No way!" Gordon states bluntly.

Dianne lowers her gaze as she mutters, "Don't tell me you actually believe the lies you've been fed all of your life."

"But how?" Gordon presses, adding, "It's not possible."

Dianne stares at Gordon in silence for a moment, then finally, after debating what to share, says, "The water filtration plant your dome used to use, failed due to sabotage. It was our people who stopped the attackers from destroying the main dome, although they did damage the outer shell."

"But where are they now?" Gordon asks warily, as it dawns on him that he had believed the Central Authority's rhetoric.

"None of the warring factions are able to do much anymore, but when they do, it's usually catastrophic." She replies. Thoughts of Aqua bring her close to tears, but she holds them back.

Miranda casts her gaze around the chamber as she says, "But to fight, now? That's just stupid! What's left to fight over?"

Dianne sighs, then says, "Pete will answer your questions tomorrow. But first, he'll show you to your quarters."

Joe feels out of place and is baffled as to why he is with the group. Glancing around, his curiosity gets the better of him, so he asks, "Dianne, why am I here?"

"I want you to save someone for me." Dianne replies with a slight waver in her voice.

Joe's face twitches as he stammers, "I dealt with stocks, not with…" he pauses, then after a hard swallow, says, "not with whatever it is you want me to do."

Dianne steps forward and places a hand on his shoulder as she says, "You have more courage in you than you realize, and once you learn of what I wish for you to do, I hope you volunteer."

Before anyone can say anything else, Pete firmly states, "There will be time for questions later on, but for now, let's get you three situated."

Dianne smiles thinly as she steps back, then hurries away before her hidden emotions break through. *He must find her!* She thinks as a tear sneaks from the corner of her eye, to roll down her cheek, it is soon followed by another. Those who protect her, ignore her tears out of respect.

Pete watches her leave, then turns to the group, and says, "Follow me."

Joe trails behind Gordon and Miranda, conscious of the soldiers which follow them.

As they walk, Gordon glances to Miranda and quietly says, "I had no idea about any of this."

Miranda is too dumbfounded to respond, instead she stares at the metal walkways. They are rusty and flaky, and obviously have been there for a long time, as has everything she sees. She looks at the tunnel they drove through and wonders how the gas does not enter. Glancing at the soldiers and vehicles, she lowers her head, ashamed. Living in the lap of luxury at the resort, she was worried about having her mind wiped, while these people's very lives are at stake.

Joe feels subdued; his whole life's work has been a sham. He lifts his head up as he decides that no longer will his life be wasted away, and vows to make a difference. He will help Dianne; in whatever it is she wants him to do.

Dianne watches them via monitors as they are assigned rooms, and although she intuitively trusts them, until they have truly proven themselves, they will be under constant guard.

Joe is used to a more spartan existence than Miranda or Gordon, thus he finds the accommodations less of a shock. A large archway connects the kitchen-dining area to the bedroom, off which a bathroom with corner shower is accessed through a sliding door. The simple layout is space-efficient, while providing each occupant a private area.

Early each evening a mass meal is prepared and served in a communal hall. People either eat in the mess-hall or return to their quarters. The three new arrivals are escorted to the hall, where they sit together.

Gordon scrunches up his face as a soupy mix of food spills from his spoon back into his bowl. "It doesn't even smell good." He laments as he leans over his bowl.

Miranda puts a small portion in her mouth, then after swallowing the soup-mix, drinks two mouthfuls of water.

Joe sighs, "It can't be that bad." He says as he motions around the room where people are eating with gusto.

Gordon slops more from his spoon into his bowl as he replies, "You can have mine as seconds if you like."

Joe takes a large spoonful, stuffs it in his mouth, and instantly regrets it. The food tastes awful, and smells musty, like the area they walked through to get to Pete's vehicle. He gags as he swallows the food, then almost knocks his water over in his haste to get a drink.

"Careful," A guard warns, "that's your daily water ration."

"Daily!" Joe exclaims as he looks at the mug, which suddenly looks too small.

Another chuckles, then says, "You'll get used to it. It's all we have."

Gordon glances up as he says, "But why can't you make it taste better? Surely there has to be a way?"

The guard sits down and rests his weapon against the table as he replies, "My name's Jerry." He waves a hand around as he continues, "It's no great secret that this place was designed to house and feed a couple of thousand, at best. But somehow, twenty-three thousand survive here, plus we deliver fresh, clean water, to your people."

Gordon stares at his food guiltily, then says, "You guys eat like this, and yet give us fresh water!"

Jerry nods to the plate and says, "That's a recent thing, it used to taste better." He continues, "Yours is not the only community we help. We also provide security and basic essentials for Aqua."

Joe tilts his head as he asks, "You call this place Golem One, and there is Aqua. So, does that mean there are other places?"

"There used to be dozens of subterranean bases, along with numerous underwater facilities." Jerry replies, then he grins as he states authoritatively, "There was even one on the moon."

"That's just old propaganda." Another soldier replies.

"It's true," Jerry insists, adding, "I heard 'em talking about the old rocket program in main ops… once." He finishes softly.

The standing soldiers shake their heads dismissively.

Jerry presses, "It's true I tell you! You'll see. One day, you'll see."

Gordon gazes around the room, then reluctantly begins eating his soup. He drinks his water conservatively in the process, and eventually empties his plate. Miranda considers her old life, and although the soup tastes horrible, she finishes hers as well.

While they eat, Jerry continues, "This place is called Golem One for a reason. It's our last holdout." He glances to his colleagues, then says, "There used to be eight other places, like this one."

"Here comes the boss!" states one of the standing soldiers as he flicks his eyes away from the table.

Jerry takes his weapon and stands with his colleagues as Dianne and her protective entourage approaches.

She stops a few steps away and says, "You three come with me. I've something to show you." She nods to the three soldiers as she turns and walks away.

Joe frowns as he stands and follows her. She clearly gave the soldiers some kind of message with her nod, but he is unable to figure out what, especially since they are still escorting them.

Dianne leads them onto a huge platform which is recessed into a wall. She firmly holds onto one of the handful of poles which jut up from the floor and waits. Her personal guard does not step onto the platform, instead they form a protective perimeter nearby, and wait. The soldiers with Joe, Gordon, and Miranda, however, do follow.

Once everyone is on the platform, Jerry shifts a large lever to one side. Massive gears, with worn down edges, begin to grind as they reluctantly turn, lifting them alongside the cliff wall. The gears are old and noisy, yet faithfully trundle them upward.

Dianne motions as she states, "Our control tower."

The elevator snugly enters a previously unnoticed hole in the ceiling and keeps climbing. Lights flicker from the top of the poles, casting ominous shadows on the walls as they continue upward. Finally, with a resounding clunk, the elevator stops.

Dianne strides from the platform into a huge, round room, then stops as she motions for them to look. The room is a miniature dome, with windows through which they see a concrete wall. Eight men and women sit at computer terminals; they each acknowledge Dianne, but remain seated, and continue with their duties.

"Show them." Dianne instructs.

Massive concrete segments lift away from the windows, allowing sunlight to filter in through dirty glass. Gordon, Miranda and Joe are awed by the sight. The room rests above the mist, atop a mountain, and provides a panoramic view of the landscape in all directions.

Dianne directs their attention inland, pointing as she states, "That's your old home, Canfield."

Joe looks at the distant, yet huge dome rising out of the mist. He frowns as something odd comes to mind, then blurts, "Hey. How is it that I could not tell where the wall inside Canfield ended, and the sky began?"

Gordon glances to Dianne, then when she says nothing, replies, "The inside of the main dome was constructed using colored cement. As for why, I can only guess that the designers wanted it to look like sky. The inside of the other, smaller domes, is fully augmented."

"Smaller domes?" Joe questions, then says, "You mentioned that before."

Dianne steps to one of the windows, and as she points, says, "Look carefully, and you can even see the holiday resort dome where Gordon and Miranda worked. It's connected by that tunnel." She adds, then pointing farther into the distance adds, "That's the seaside resort dome, amongst others."

"I'm still getting used to the idea that I didn't live where I thought I did." Joe replies.

Dianne turns her attention to the water and says, "And out there is Aqua, and without its water filtration systems, we're all dead."

The room goes quiet at her blunt statement.

Miranda swallows hard at Dianne's comment, then stares wide-eyed as she listens.

Gordon feels a chill run through his body at her words, and says, "Dead? Why'd you bring us here then?"

Dianne turns to the three of them and says, "We don't know what happened. What we do know is that there was an earthquake, and then we lost contact, along with the water, which stopped flowing."

Miranda's jaw drops as she says, "Which means that no one gets fresh water."

"Correct." Dianne replies, then says, "At best, we have a month's supply."

The people at the terminals keep glancing back and forth, as if apprehensive.

Gordon feels tension building in the room, and says, "What are you not telling us?"

Dianne looks at Joe for a moment, then says, "My daughter, Maggie, was visiting Aqua when we lost contact."

Joe's jaw drops as he asks, "Why not send your people? You have lots!"

Dianne gazes outside as she replies, "Because if she is being held hostage by a hostile faction, I will need someone they would never expect, to rescue her."

Gordon lifts his hands as he says apprehensively, "When did this become a hostage situation? I thought it was an earthquake?"

"We don't know what caused the quake." Dianne replies slowly, "It could have been a natural event, or an attack, and we'll only get one chance to find out."

Gordon steps back as he says, "And you want us to go?"

Joe steps forward as he states, "I'll go."

Dianne lowers her gaze as relief causes a tear to sneak out of the corner of her eye. She replies, "Joe, thank you."

She lifts her gaze to Gordon and says, "This is the plan. You three have just escaped from Canfield and have fled into the ocean to avoid detection, using a vehicle you found in one of Canfield's bays."

Gordon frowns as he interrupts, "But why us? You have people trained for this kind of stuff?"

Dianne pauses for a moment, then replies, "When we received your request for extraction, I saw a unique opportunity. We saved you from having your minds wiped, and hopefully, in return, you'll help us."

Gordon shakes his head as he repeats, "But how are we to do this?"

Dianne continues, "Following a distress beacon, you'll locate Aqua. Once there, if the facility has been taken by hostiles, you three will not be killed on sight, but questioned instead."

"Great, we get captured!" Gordon states bluntly.

Dianne offers a slim smile as she replies, "If Aqua is gone, you will know, and return here. If the facility is intact, and safe, you will return here with Maggie, and news as to what's going on."

She pauses as her expression hardens, "And if we don't hear from you for two days; that's when we send an offensive force."

Miranda frowns as she asks, "But surely you sent someone to investigate as soon as this happened?"

"We did, and we haven't heard from them since they went underwater." Dianne replies.

Gordon frowns, then says, "Then attack. They were obviously captured!"

"If Aqua is not flooded, then any attack risks them all." She stares hard at Gordon as she presses, "But, you three will be approaching from Canfield, along with reports of being pursued."

Gordon sighs, then says, "I get it." He lowers his head as he mumbles, "I'll go."

Miranda stares at Gordon, then asks, "And you want me to go, because I'm just a silly woman who worked in a holiday resort."

Dianne motions to Miranda as she says, "I mean no insult, but the three of you have clearly lived easy lives. You're not overweight, but, obviously none of you are going short either, plus your hands are the true giveaway, they're soft. Add to this your unease around weapons; clearly you're not military, which means that you three make a perfect infiltration team." She puts her hands on her hips as she finishes with a smile.

Gordon motions to the room as he asks, "But aren't you worried about spies?"

Dianne laughs, the unexpected sound reverberates loudly around the room. She gets a grip on herself as she says, "See! You three are perfect. You have no idea how it is out here. I love it."

The three of them glance at each other, perplexed, but none of them say anything.

Aqua

Gordon, Miranda, and Joe are given a quick lesson on how to operate the cramped vehicle. They are all uneasy with how old it looks. Rust flakes off its body, while many of its window seals look as though they have been patched multiple times. Its six tires are worn out, as are the four seats inside.

Jerry motions to the floor as he says, "The batteries are almost new, and have a full charge. Plus, if you get above the mist, the solar panels will still provide a little power."

Joe closes his eyes as he recalls their instructions, then says, "Well, let's get going."

Gordon glances at Joe nervously, then says, "I'm not in so much of a hurry to drown in this contraption." He then turns to Jerry and says, "So, we're to travel along the coast until we reach a point near the old road that leads to Canfield."

Jerry nods, then says, "Then you enter the water, push that button, which converts the drive to water mode, and you're all set."

Miranda gazes at the control panel, and then says, "And this brings up the map, where we will *discover* Aqua, and then head to it in the hopes they help us."

Jerry grins as he replies, "Perfect!"

Joe has been wondering about the various factions, and asks, "Why do we call your people Subverts, and what is the name given to the people you're at war with?"

Jerry nods wistfully as he replies, "Well, to answer your second question first, it's not one faction we are at war with. There's only a hand full of true societies left, scattered around, and for the most part, we all help each other, when we can. But, there are groups which survive by taking what they need, and when they do, they often destroy the communities they encounter."

Gordon quizzes, "Can't you just wipe them out?"

"Simply put," Jerry replies, "we don't have the manpower, or the supplies to do that."

Joe motions to Jerry's weapon, which rests nearby, and says, "That looks like something you guys manufacture."

Jerry sighs as he replies, "No, that weapon is older than my father, and was handed to him from his father, along with instructions on how to replace the components as they wear out."

Miranda stares at Jerry, and as the hair on the back of her neck rises, she asks, "What happens to the old people?"

Jerry grins as he replies, "It's not what you think. We have vast farms, and recycling facilities, which require a lot of people to maintain. When we're too old and slow to be on the front line, we hand our weapon to the next generation, and do what we can to benefit the rest." He lifts his head high as he says, "My father still lives, and works in metal scrap."

Miranda relaxes, it was beginning to sound as if they killed them off, or worse.

Joe presses, "I'm still curious as to why you're called Subverts. It doesn't make a lot of sense."

Jerry shrugs as he replies, "That's why I answered your second question first, I really have no idea."

Gordon lifts his hands as if lost, and offers, "Subterranean…" He pauses then says, "I don't know."

Joe shakes his head as he shares his thoughts, "I'm still unclear as to why the Central Authority would want to keep us all in the dark about the truth."

"That's simple." Gordon replies, "If the citizens think there is plenty to go around, there won't be a rebellion. Plus, look at how busy everyone is in the city. It's all about the stock market, sports, and anything else but the dwindling resources."

Joe sighs deeply, "You're right. People would riot, and then what? If they tried to go outside…" he lets the words trail off.

Jerry glances at the console, frowns, then says, "Oh no. You have to go now! Once you're underwater you should pick up Aqua's beacon." He flicks a series of switches, then pauses as he rechecks everything. He stares at the three of them as he states with urgency, "Hurry!"

Gordon scrutinizes the console, but is unable to figure out what Jerry saw that made him abruptly end their session. He swallows nervously as he says, "Okay, let's do this."

Jerry leaves the vehicle, then watches as they secure the entry, as instructed, and then drive off. He smiles thinly as the vehicle meanders back and forth, then begins to follow a straighter path. Once they are out of sight, he activates a previously hidden communicator, and says, "Dianne, they're on the road."

"Good," Dianne replies, then says, "I take it you saw the alert?"

"I did, and I disabled it." Jerry replies, "I don't see the need for them to have any additional

84

concerns. Besides, the water should afford them some protection, if they make it in time."

"Seal the entrance." Dianne orders, then looking out from the control tower at the ocean, orders, "Seal everything, enable full protection protocol."

She watches as the concrete slabs lower over the windows, then feels the entire control tower sink as her orders are followed. Somewhere out there, a nuclear bomb just detonated. Dianne wonders if it was an accident, intentional, or simply an old weapon exploding by itself.

Meanwhile, on the coastal road, Miranda shoves Gordon out of the control chair, stating bluntly, "I don't know what it is with you boys, but you can't drive!"

The combination of hand and foot controls, with the myriad of switches, had the two overthinking men perplexed, while Miranda simply operates the vehicle as if born to do it. With her at the controls, they begin to make great time.

"What's that?" Joe asks as he points to a red-tinged cloud which rolls their way across the ocean.

The closer it gets, the greater their concern. With the cloud, a tidal wave of debris rolls toward them.

"Go inland." Gordon nervously instructs.

"No!" Miranda replies, then asks, "Have you ever been to the beach, the holiday beach?"

"Ah, no." Gordon admits as he stares fearfully at the fast approaching wave. "I don't see what your vacation has to do with this predicament." He states, his voice reaching a higher pitch.

Miranda applies full power as she swings them toward the receding water. "We'll be safe if we can dive under that wave!"

Joe sits in the chair next to Miranda and buckles the restraints. Gordon hurries to do the same, his breathing becomes short as fear overtakes him. The water is retreating almost as fast as they are driving, leaving behind mounds of junk and debris, adding to Miranda's difficulties. She cusses to herself as she swerves back and forth around the piles of garbage. The familiar blue-green mist hovers, swirling around as though a living thing. The soggy sand drags at their undercarriage as they sink deeper.

"Damn it!" Miranda shouts as she intentionally drives them over the garbage, adding to Gordon's fears. Unseen objects bang and clang along the underside of the vehicle but provides them with much needed traction.

"We're going to make it!" Joe shouts as they begin to catch the retreating water.

Gordon moans as he points, his finger shaking from fear. They are catching the water, but only because it is now surging back toward them, bringing with it a wall of debris which is partially obscured by the mist.

Miranda's hand is poised over the controls which transition them from a ground vehicle to a watercraft. Water splashes at the front window, bringing with it chunks of rubbish which smashes hard against the glass. Just as they feel the craft getting lifted, she flicks the switches. A low hum emanates from below and behind them as turbines which have remained unused for a long time, engage.

They bob above the surface for a brief moment, and stare at the massive wall of water which approaches. Miranda pushes them forward, and down, keeping them as close to the bottom as she can. Miraculously, they slide below the layer of garbage, and into water mostly free of obstacles, where they pick up speed.

Suddenly it happens, the tidal wave rolls overhead. The swift current pushes them backward and threatens to tumble them over. Then it passes, leaving them able to maneuver. Miranda does not hesitate, and as the continental plate dips, she turns the exterior lights on, and dives them into the ocean depths. The unexpected stillness of the water is unnerving at first, but still a great relief compared to the rough entry they experienced.

"What was that?" Gordon questions.

Joe tilts his head as he says, "I think Jerry knew something was wrong."

Miranda stares at a blinking light on the console but says nothing as she switches off the radiation warning. She wonders who even has, let alone uses, radioactive weapons. It is not as if people can live outdoors anyway. Then she wonders if the entire planet is really like this, or if some areas are better, perhaps even habitable.

Descending deeper, they all become quiet in the eerie depths. The blast wave reaches Canfield, its near spent energies wash over the outer dome, and other than a few more support girders falling to the ground between the domes, little else happens. Most of the inhabitants are oblivious to the blast, while the few who do know of the incident, wish they did not.

Meanwhile, in the ocean depths, something huge unexpectedly swims past the front window of the rescue vehicle. Miranda slows them down as the three of them stare into the shadowy waters. Something bumps into them, again and again. Each bump harder than the previous.

Miranda nervously says, "I think we know what happened to the last team that came this way. Whatever that thing is, it doesn't seem to like us."

A huge shadow moves past the front window, then turns their way, its dull white eyes seem to stare at them lifelessly. Its tooth-filled, wide-open jaw, could easily swallow them whole.

Joe turns to Gordon and says, "I thought you said there was nothing living left."

Gordon shakily points as he states, "Well, that's not a bloody squirrel is it!"

Miranda engages full reverse as she attempts to turn them away from the gaping maw. The creature's teeth scrape along their vehicle, sounding like nails on a chalkboard as it grinds down the side of their transport. She shuts off the thrusters and lights, then says, "I think it's attracted to our noise, or lights, or both."

With their thrusters off, they begin to sink into the darkness. The minutes pass tensely, but the watery beast does not return. As they sink, a strange popping sound resounds from the vehicle as it compresses in the pressure, causing their ears to pop.

Miranda quickly looks at the instrument panel, the soft glow of their lights reveals her stress in the deep lines on her face.

"We're too deep!" She exclaims shrilly.

Gordon and Joe do not say anything, they can both see that she is doing the best she can, and as neither of them have any ideas, they simply wait, and hope.

Miranda peers into the gloomy depths, fearfully, but is unable to discern anything. Reluctantly, she turns on their thrusters, then sets them to the lowest setting. After a moment, their motion arrests their descent, then slowly lifts them out of the trench they were sinking into.

Just as Miranda breathes a sigh of relief, a monstrous sea creature, perhaps the same one, swims past them. It propels them to one side, then it is gone. With her heart racing, she notices an odd shimmering near the window. Running her fingers along the window seal, she is alarmed when they come away wet.

Quickly glancing to Gordon and Joe, she sees they are too intent on peering into the gloomy depths to notice the water seeping in. She focuses her attention on the console, with particular interest on the map which shows their location. They continue onward, until finally reaching where Aqua is supposed to be. They slowly crisscross the area, searching.

Miranda stares into the dark depths and says, "I can't see any lights, or anything."

"They said we'd pick up a beacon!" Joe states, then in frustration says, "Let's turn the lights on. We have to see; this wandering around blindly is not helping us."

Hesitantly, Miranda turns the outside lights on, and gasps at the sight.

Aqua is a ruined mess. Of the dozen domes which constitute the facility, only three appear intact, and they are dark.

"Shut your lights off!" Screeches a voice from the vehicle's speakers.

Miranda immediately shuts them off, and the thrusters, then waits. Something large swims close by, causing them to wallow in its wake.

After a few moments Miranda flicks the communications channel, and says, "This is Miranda, from, um…" She turns to Gordon and Joe and says, "I think we should tell them the truth. It looks to me as though the sea creatures are to blame for all of this."

Both men nod in agreement, then Miranda continues, "This is Miranda, on a rescue mission from Golem One, how can we help?"

"As slowly as you can, approach landing bay nine." The voice replies.

Miranda shrugs, then replies, "I have no idea where that is."

"Hang on!" The voice retorts, clearly annoyed. A moment later the voice returns, "I will flash a light over the entryway twice, and twice only."

"Okay." Miranda replies, then waits.

"Down there!" Joe says, pointing at a faint flicker of light.

Gordon squints, then shakes his head as he says, "I didn't see anything."

Miranda turns their thrusters onto the lowest setting, and heads for the location Joe indicated. After a few moments they approach a concrete overhang, and slowly glide under it. The overhang leads to a tunnel, which after a short distance ends at a blank wall.

"I have to cycle it through slowly." States the voice from the speakers.

After what feels like an eternity, the water drains away as the floor lifts them into a hangar bay. A small group of people are waiting for them, including a young girl.

Gordon, Joe, and Miranda step out of the vehicle, their ears popping once more. Miranda glances back to the vehicle and is surprised to see metal shining through the paint where the creature's teeth dug a series of grooves along the hull.

Joe smiles as he recognizes the girl and says, "Your mom sent us to find out what happened here."

An elderly man steps forward as he replies, "Those bloody fish is what happened!"

"Now, now." Another man interjects, "It was the Earthquake which severed the water and communication lines, along with collapsing three of our modules."

"Well, the bloody fish came after that and did the rest!" The old man insists angrily.

"Yes, the fish." The other man agrees, then motions as he says, "We're being rude. I'm Ken, this is Andrew, Julie, Demetri, Brett, and young Maggie."

Gordon motions as he replies, "I'm Gordon, and these are my friends, Miranda and Joe."

Joe smiles as he takes steps forward and says, "Maggie, I feel as though I already know you."

Maggie looks up at Joe, and trustingly takes his hand as she pleads, "Are you here to help us?"

Joe turns to Gordon and Miranda as he replies, "We'll take you back to your mom, along with a list of what is needed to repair this place."

"What about those fish?" Demands the old man, who Ken introduced as Demetri.

Miranda narrows her eyes as she questions, "Did you say if they arrived after the earthquake, or after you activated your emergency beacon?"

Ken frowns, then says, "Well, it's hard to say. We activated the beacon as soon as the quake hit, and the fish showed up a little after that."

"I wonder if we can draw them away?" Miranda asks.

"But won't they just come back?" Demetri asks as he places his hands on his hips.

91

"I don't think so," Miranda replies, "wherever they came from, they must have had a lot of food, and there doesn't seem to be any out there for them."

Gordon recalls the trash covered ocean as he asks, "But where?"

Miranda smiles as she replies positively, "Some parts of the planet must be recovering."

"Well that's just great!" Demetri grouches.

"Think about it." Miranda presses, "You process fresh water from down here, which means that only the surface is contaminated."

Julie gasps, then says, "Oh my. We missed it all along. The oxygenation levels have been on the rise for years! We thought it was a localized event due to our filtration efforts."

Ken lifts his hand as he stops the conversation, and says, "Before we get ahead of ourselves, first things first." He glances around at the others, then continues, "We have eighty-six survivors, out of nine hundred forty-seven. The filtration facility is flooded, and the pipework to the coast damaged. It would take a miracle to get this place up and running again, and we're fresh out of miracles."

Gordon puts his hand to his chin as he considers a crazy idea, then with a wide smile says, "The auto-fixers! We need them."

Joe frowns as he recalls Henry's comment about fixers being replaced by machines. He gulps as he says, "Henry was concerned about us not being able to repair things. But how does getting one of those machines help us?"

Gordon grins, "Henry knew a lot. I bet he anticipated the need, and…" He trails off as he frowns, then says, "You know, I have no idea where Henry went, no-one does."

Miranda tilts her head as she says, "Henry was able to anticipate and predict events with great accuracy. Is it possible that, somehow, he foresaw this disaster?"

Joe's frown deepens as he says, "But how?"

Gordon shakes his head slowly as he says, "Henry was always a step ahead of everyone else. But, I don't think he foresaw this disaster, as much as he anticipated the need to repair the aging systems out here."

Ken shakes his head as he interrupts again, saying, "This is all well and good. But can we have this discussion above water? We need to get out of here!"

"Right!" Gordon replies, then says, "We should leave right away, and come back with as many rescue vehicles as we can."

Miranda nods, "Running slow, the fish seemed to ignore us."

Ken fumbles in his pocket, then handing Gordon a handful of notes, says, "I put together a brief list of what we need, if we're to repair this place." he looks around, his expression indicating that he thinks the task is hopeless.

Gordon flicks through the list then asks, "How about your own transports? I would have expected you to have an abundance."

Ken shakes his head as he replies, "That module was the first the fish destroyed. I think all the thruster activity and lights attracted them."

Demetri interrupts, "Nope. The fish smashed the beacon first, then took out the transport module."

Gordon has been thinking. He steps closer to Joe, who still holds Maggie's hand, then says, "I think Henry wanted us to leave the city."

Joe shakes his head in confusion as he replies, "I have no idea what you're going on about?"

"Henry knew about the auto-fixers." Gordon states as he puts together all he knows, then says, "He wasn't worried about them taking over. He wanted me to know about them, and used you to get the message to me."

"But why?" Joe asks, still confused.

"Because I have contact with the outside, and because out here, we can use the technology." Gordon replies

Miranda interrupts them with a glare as she growls, "Let's go!"

Once the three of them, plus Maggie, are aboard their vehicle, they are lowered back into the water.

Miranda leaves their lights off, and moves them out slowly. She closes her eyes as she operates the vehicle, moving them up and away from the smashed facility by memory alone. As they move into open water she opens her eyes and breathes a sigh of relief. Keeping them at a slow pace, she adjusts their heading, and makes for the coast. A thin veil of light filters through to them, but does little more than change the color of the water; their visibility is still essentially zero.

Gordon is unable to get his mind off Henry, which is a good thing. If he had seen Miranda piloting with her eyes closed, he would have had a panic attack. He frowns as he mumbles, "Heck, now that I think about it, I don't even know where he worked."

Joe glances to Gordon and says, "Is it important? He worked with me, if you really want to know."

Gordon shakes his head, he knows he is onto something, but is unable to figure it out. He keeps replaying the events which led up to this point, but each time he ends up with too many unknowns.

As the craft rises in the water, light begins to filter in from the outside, revealing the flotsam filled, murky waters they are now familiar with. Miranda stares at the radiation meter, then notices that the levels detected, though higher than before, are not lethal to them. Every now and then she glances at the window seal, wishing each time she did not, as water droplets continue to leak through. She says nothing to the others, instead, focusing on the task of getting them safely to land.

Maggie squeals with delight as Miranda surfs the waves to the shore, successfully dodging most of the larger debris, while the smaller objects are brushed aside.

Miranda is keen to get out of the water, and engages the land mode a little too early, causing them to drift and flounder. Sweat beads on her forehead as she battles the near useless controls. Finally, the wheels make contact with the sandy bottom, allowing them to forge their way up the beach. As they climb away from the waves, the mist thins, all but fading to nothing as they reach the coast road.

"That was fun!" Maggie giggles as she leans forward, holding onto Joe's hand.

Miranda wipes her sweaty palms, then quickly reviews the map. She relaxes; they are much closer to Golem One than she had expected them to be. She glances at the window seal, where little bubbles of air and water pop. Recalling Jerry's instructions, she increases their cabin pressure slightly, making a mental note to get it looked at when they get back.

As soon as the long tunnel comes into view, Maggie squeals excitedly, bobbing up and down in her chair. "We're home!" She cheers.

Dianne is waiting, not so patiently, as she paces back and forth; she had received word that they were returning and anxiously watched their progress from the control tower. As soon as the vehicle enters the tunnel, she relaxes a little, then heads to meet them. The lift is still trundling downward as the vehicle swings into view, causing her heart to flutter. As they get closer, she spots her daughter waving through the window and breathes a sigh of relief.

Miranda parks near Dianne, then opens the door.

"You could have sent word!" Dianne chastises as the four of them get out.

Maggie rushes to Dianne, and hugs her tightly as she breaks down, "It was so scary; all I could hear was water rushing in from everywhere."

Dianne soothes her, "You're safe now!"

"I was supposed to be on a floater, but the pilot left without me." Maggie sobs as held back emotions overcome her.

Dianne's lip's quiver; had Maggie been on any of the escaping vehicles, she would probably be dead by now.

Gordon steps forward with Ken's list in hand and opens his mouth to speak, but stops when Dianne flicks a resolute look his way. She waves him off, saying, "We'll discuss Aqua in the control tower, in a little while."

Jerry approaches the group, and with a huge grin states, "I knew you'd make it!"

Gordon smiles as he replies, "I hope I don't have to go back, that's for sure."

Nodding to the notes in Gordon's hand, Jerry asks, "What's that?"

"A repair list for Aqua." He replies.

"Let's find Pete." Jerry offers, "He'll know what to do with that."

The two of them discuss the underwater trek as they wander off, with Gordon embellishing his role

Walking to the back of the vehicle, Joe runs his fingers along the groove the fish made with its teeth as he walks forward. He frowns as his fingers reach the front, where a tooth rests, embedded into the window seal. He turns to Miranda, who upon seeing his horrified gaze, purses her lips and shrugs. They both hurriedly glance to the retreating Gordon, then pass a knowing look, which says they will not tell him about it.

Miranda had not noticed the tooth before, otherwise she would not have risked the return trip without getting it repaired. She stands next to Joe as he wiggles it loose. It falls into his hand, filing his palm with its size.

"It's damn heavy too!" Joe states, then presenting the tooth to Miranda, states, "A trophy for you."

She takes the offered tooth and turns it over in her hands. It is large, with a blunt point, while the sides have small serrated edges. "This looks like it's designed to rip flesh from other fish." She says.

Joe glances up the ramp as he subconsciously considers the vast ocean. He swallows hard as he asks, "What else is out there that is large enough for that thing to feed on?"

"Let's hope we don't find out!" Miranda replies, already assuming they are going back.

He picks up her demeanor, then stammers, "Why would we go back?"

She motions to Maggie and Dianne, then says, "For them."

Joe offers a thin smile as he replies with equal conviction, "Yes."

As they continue talking, a soldier inspects the damage where the tooth was removed. He acknowledges the pair with a nod, then wanders off to find a repair technician.

A few hours pass before Gordon, Joe, and Miranda, are summoned to the control tower. Once more they ride the aging elevator upward, then arriving at the tower they see Dianne talking with two older people

"Ah, you're here," Dianne says, then before they can reply introduces the pair, "Stephanie and Scott are from the ruling council. We're discussing how we can effect repairs to the water filtration system."

"Oh," Miranda says, "I thought you were in charge?"

Dianne chuckles, "Of this tower yes, but of Golem One as a whole, ah, no."

Gordon grins as he says, "As soon I saw the damage, I thought of the auto-fixers from Canfield."

Joe recalls Gordon's comments at the time, then nods in agreement.

"What caused that explosion?" Miranda interrupts as she puts her hands on her hips. "It was radioactive!"

Dianne waves through the open windows as she replies, "Our sources tell us it was an old stockpile which blew."

"Well, the timing couldn't have been any worse." She retorts.

Dianne stares outside wistfully, then says, "They blow up more often than you think. That's why the world is still such a mess."

"Can't you do something about them?" Miranda asks.

Dianne slowly shakes her head as she says, "All we can do is mark where stockpiles of old weapons and nuclear reactors are, and then avoid the areas."

Stephanie lifts her hand up as she says, "Our priority here today, is the repair of the water filtration systems on Aqua." She motions to Gordon and says, "What are these auto-fixers?"

Gordon smiles as he replies, "Henry drew our attention to the auto-fixers when he told Joe about them."

Joe recalls that day and shake his head, "Made a scene you mean. I'm sure he had other ways to tell you about them, without involving me!"

"I'm glad he did." Dianne replies with a soft smile.

Miranda tilts her head as she replays the events that led up to them being where they are, then gasps, "We were pretty much told to leave Canfield, and to come out here."

Gordon shakes his head as he says, "But why? We could have coordinated meetings from where we were."

Dianne steps forward and puts a hand on his shoulder as she says, "It's one thing to learn of our situation out here. But until you actually see it, and experience it, would you really know? How much would you have risked, to help us?"

Miranda lowers her gaze as she mumbles, "I had it easy, too easy. I wouldn't have believed it, and I would have turned a blind eye to all of this."

"So, Henry manipulated events to get you all out here, to see the real world." Dianne replies, then with a frown adds, "Yet he remains inside Canfield. Why?"

Gordon grinds his jaw as he ponders the question, then snorts as he replies, "I bet he wasn't sure if you really needed help or not. The whole thing could have all been a ploy by the Central Authority!" He waves his arms to indicate himself, Joe and Miranda as he continues, "And while he is a key member, we're expendable."

Miranda's jaw drops as she quips, "Which means he is waiting to see what happens.

Stephanie shakes her head as she interrupts, "This drivel is not getting us anywhere."

Dianne frowns as she replies, "I'm not so sure." She motions to Gordon as she instructs, "Go on."

"I've got it!" Joe shouts, unexpectedly loudly. He stares at Gordon as he explains, "We used to move stocks, and watch the market trends." With a grin he says, "Applying that thinking to our situation is no different. Henry gave a little push to me, thus distracting the market, I mean the Central Authority, from the real transaction."

"Transaction?" Miranda questions.

"Yes" Joe states, then looking at Gordon he feels a chill run up the back of his neck as he says, "Henry is making a big move! But what would be big enough to lose the resort over? That's what we have to figure out. What's the trade off?"

"Water!" Gordon replies.

Dianne frowns as she counters, "The quake had not yet happened when he started all this. So how?"

"Henry was a long-term markets man." Joe replies, recalling the projects they worked on. "And to my understanding, Aqua was our only water source." With a grin he states, "Henry learned of these new auto-fixers, and was concerned that we would lose the ability to repair the systems."

Miranda shakes her head in confusion as she asks, "Why wouldn't they know?"

Gordon gasps, "Because Canfield has no water-systems to repair. Therefore, they would not have been programmed for anything more than simple pipe repairs…"

"PIPE REPAIRS!" Joe and Miranda shout in unison, interrupting Gordon.

Dianne folds her arms as she turns to Stephanie and says, "I think this has been rather productive!"

Scott glances to Stephanie, then says, "Dianne, you'll have whatever you need to get that water flowing."

Gordon stares into the distance at Canfield's damaged outer dome, then with mounting apprehension says, "We have to go back inside and get a message to my contacts."

Miranda sighs as she says, "I'll go with you."

"Don't count me out!" Joe states, "I'm coming too."

Dianne glances to the three of them, then says, "Pete will drop you off, then go back and pick you up once you're ready. While you're gone, we'll figure out a way to get rid of those large fish and evacuate Aqua, until we can repair the pipework."

"The beacon!" Miranda, states, then explains, "The fish were attracted to the distress beacon. If you can make one and attach it to something to lure them away, you should be good to go."

Dianne nods as she states, "Good. It looks like we have a plan!" She relaxes a little, then ponders. Luckily for Aqua, each dome has its own air-filtration unit. With there being less than one hundred survivors, they have a little time, perhaps even a few weeks before the air becomes too stale to be filtered. She recalls the old oxygenators Aqua used to use and decides that they should get put back into service. They should never have been reliant on Golem One for air. She shakes her head as she walks to the control tower.

Canfield

Pete stares at his three passengers and shakes his head. Gordon is sitting with his legs crossed, clearly nervous, while Joe appears to be looking forward to going. However, he is unable to tell if Miranda is apprehensive about reentering the dome.

The trek back to Canfield feels shorter than when they departed, and the closer they get, the quieter and more subdued they become. The thrill of the adventure has lost its excitement as the reality that they may get caught sinks in.

Pete uses bay nineteen this time; opening an outer door in the dome is always nerve wracking. "Here we go." He states apprehensively. He is sure that one of these times he will open the entryway to find a line of Canfield's auto-cops waiting for him.

They all relax when they get inside, unopposed. Pete shuts the outer door; then waits for the gas which flowed in with them to dissipate before opening the vehicle's door.

As Gordon, Joe, and Miranda exit, Pete waves and says, "Good luck! I'll come back for you after you signal."

Joe looks around, then frowns as he asks, "How do we get to the city?"

"We don't" Gordon replies.

Miranda grabs Joe's arm as she says, "C'mon, let's get out of here, so Pete can leave."

Gordon walks with them, and as Joe watches, he takes a device from his pocket, and quietly speaks into it.

"Of course!" Joe exclaims, "You still have your contacts."

Gordon nods as he walks ahead, still talking quietly into his device.

Pete watches them walk off, then once they are well clear of the entryway, he reopens it. The blue-green mist drifts inside as he drives out, filling the area between the domes. The gas drifts about slowly, as if a living thing, before fading away.

Joe sniffs the air apprehensively as an unpleasant odor assaults his nose. He leaves Miranda behind as he quickens his pace, even passing Gordon in his haste.

Miranda chuckles as Gordon begins sniffing as well. She then sighs as she asks the men, "If you think it's poisonous, why sniff at it?"

Joe slows as he asks, "It is deadly though, right?"

Miranda recalls asking the same question when she was at Golem One, and repeats what she learned, "It's only deadly in heavy concentrations, like outside in the lowlands. But even there, if you can get high enough, you can survive for quite a while."

Gordon narrows his eyes as he says, "Pete told us that fifteen minutes was about all someone would live."

Miranda grins as she replies, "That's true, if you were stuck, without the means to get to higher ground, like the coast road."

"That's why Golem One is okay. The entrance is above the gas!" Gordon exclaims.

Miranda nods, then shares more of what she learned, "And get this. Aqua was receiving fresh air from Golem One, while they sent fresh water back."

Joe stops as it all fits into place. Shaking his head, he says, "That's why they're evacuating. They're using up their reserve air, but once we repair the pipes, they'll get air, and all of us will get water."

Gordon agrees, "It's a vicious cycle. We all need Aqua for water, while they need Golem One for air." He pauses, then says, "But, what is Canfield needed for?"

Miranda frowns as she ponders the question, then Joe blurts out, "Population!"

Gordon stops as well, then asks, "I wonder how many other domes, like Canfield, they're helping?"

"That's a good question," Miranda replies, then tilts her head as she asks, "I wonder why we call them Subverts though? It's not as if they are doing anything subversive."

Joe shares his thoughts, "But, they know the truth, a truth that'd probably destroy this place." He shrugs as he finishes, "So they're a risk to Canfield's way of life."

Gordon grabs his device, then as he listens, grins. He is still smiling when he relays, "That was Henry! He said he'll bring six auto-fixers to gate eleven at dusk."

Joe snorts, "Dusk!"

Miranda repeats with disbelief, "Six! How did he do this?"

Gordon shrugs, "You'll have to ask him when he gets there."

They take their time getting to gate eleven, with each of them noticing that the distance between the gates varies greatly. They cautiously walk around another area where steel beams have collapsed from somewhere above.

Joe frets, "Why is this damage not being repaired?"

Gordon peers into the darkness above as he replies, "That baffles me too. I'm sure they could if they wanted to."

"So, they aren't, on purpose?" Joe questions.

"So, it seems." Gordon states bluntly. He is not annoyed with Joe, but more so with himself. For all his knowledge, he knows little of the real world, and prior to recent events, he had thought he was an important figure. With a sigh, he is realizing that he is simply a pawn, and seemingly an expendable one at that.

Auto-fixers

Henry whistles a tune as he operates the transport, driving it toward one of the few large exits from the inner dome to the service corridor. The cab has a single long bench, which is wide enough for three people. The controls are centrally mounted, and simplistic in their nature. The flat bed of the truck has six large crates strapped to it in pairs, with room for four more. Each crate is as tall as Henry and nearly as wide, causing them to hang over the sides of the transport by a good margin. He slows as he arrives, then parks facing the exit and waits. He gazes up to the sky. And even though he knows the scenery is artificial, he enjoys the sight anyway.

As the trio approaches entryway eleven, Gordon contacts Henry, "We're close. How about you?"

"I'm already here, waiting." Henry replies, distracted by the setting sun.

Gordon leads them out from the service way and smiles when he sees the transport. He waves as he says gleefully, "We're in business!"

Henry steps out from the cab, and then says, "It's good to finally meet you all."

Gordon stares at the cargo, stunned, then asks, "How did you get these?"

"You don't want to know." Henry replies, then handing Gordon a small tablet, he explains, "That has instructions on how to get these things to work.

Joe looks around, then with a frown asks, "Why did we all come? It looks like you had all of this planned out from the start."

Henry chuckles, "I wish!" He exclaims, then says, "I had no idea how this would work out, and figured it was best to involve you all, just in case."

Joe's frown deepens as he demands, "I'm confused. Why did you involve me?"

Henry nods as he replies, "You do deserve an explanation." He pauses, then gathering his thoughts, continues, "It was dumb luck really. When I saw you at the park and recognized you, it dawned on me that you would keep the Central Authority busy while I acquired these!" He pats the cargo with a smile, then narrows his eyes as he adds, "I kept tabs on you, just in case I needed to get you out, but then Gordon did that all on his own."

Joe takes a deep breath, then replies, "I should be annoyed at being used, but I'm not." He stares at Henry, then with a nod adds, "Actually, I'm glad I'm able to help!"

Miranda relaxes as they talk, then looks inside the cab of the transport, and asks, "Who's driving?"

Joe and Gordon reply simultaneously, "You are!"

Henry puts his hand on the side of one of the boxes as he says, "You guys had better get going. I don't know how long it will take you to get these to where they need to be."

Gordon shakes Henry's hand as he replies, "Thank you."

Joe looks around, perplexed, then asks, "How are you going to get back?"

"I have a transit vehicle at the next bay," Henry shrugs as he adds, "it's not too far."

The three of them leave Henry standing by the transport as they situate themselves in the cab. The inner doorway opens, causing them to freeze.

"HOLD UP!" Arnold orders from the doorway, his weapon trained on Henry's back.

Henry reluctantly raises his hands as he turns around.

"The rest of you, show yourselves." Arnold orders, his weapon unwaveringly pointed at Henry.

Reluctantly, Gordon, Miranda, and Joe step out of the transport vehicle. They also keep their hands visible, and up, as they line up next to Henry.

"You!" Arnold states as he motions to Joe, "You were a Subvert all along."

"There are no Subverts." Joe replies blandly.

"Then what are you?" Arnold demands.

Joe sighs as he replies, "Just people who are trying to get the water fixed."

"Fixed?" Arnold questions, then states, "Your people are probably the ones responsible for the bacteria in the dam."

"Dam?" Joe questions, surprised.

"Yes, where we get our drinking water! Did you suddenly get stupid from being out there?" Arnold states, his weapon now pointed at Joe.

Henry sighs as he replies, "There's no dam. That's just another lie."

A dark vehicle appears in the distance, and approaches at high speed, causing all of them to become agitated. Henry glances to his colleagues as he shrugs, indicating he has no idea who is coming.

Arnold positions himself so that he can cover his captives, while keeping a watchful eye on the speeding vehicle. Sweat builds in his armpits as the tension mounts.

Moments later, the vehicle stops. Doctor Liang gets out, and as he slowly walks to Arnold, instructs, "Let them go."

Doctor Liang looks at Henry, then smiles as he recognizes him, and then nods as he says, "Well, now I know what the emergency was."

Henry's eyes narrow as he asks, "But how'd you know?"

Liang motions to Arnold as he answers, "When he failed to turn up at a scheduled meeting, I tried to contact him. When I kept getting notified that he was dealing with an emergency situation, I looked up his bio-tracker. The moment I saw that he was out here at the edge of the dome, I knew something was going on."

"Do you know this man?" Arnold demands, motioning to Henry.

Liang chuckles as he replies, "You don't recognize senior medical director Richard *Henry* Walker?"

Arnold's gun wavers as he stares wide-eyed at Henry. "He does look similar." He admits.

Liang slowly lifts his hand, then gently pushes Arnold's gun down as he reiterates, "Just let them go."

Arnold frowns as he complies, then turning to Doctor Liang, asks, "Is there really no dam?"

Liang slowly nods as he replies, "I told you before, that we get our water from outside. And now our only water source is damaged, and these people are all we have to make it right."

Arnold stares at his identification tag, then takes it off and tosses it to the ground as he sighs, "Go!"

Henry slowly steps forward and picks up Arnold's tag. He hands it back to him as he states, "We need you to remain exactly where you are, to help these people."

"Helping outsiders is a serious crime." Arnold replies, aghast at the idea, "I would be so lucky as to only be given a memory wipe."

Henry grins as he replies, "We are the law! In fact, I do believe that you have just been promoted, to senior lead investigator of all Subvert activity. Nothing will happen without your direct knowledge, and no actions taken without your specific orders."

Arnold frowns as he takes his tag back, then asks, "But why?"

Henry motions to the dome as he replies, "Thousands depend on us to keep them safe, and if they knew the truth, they'd probably revolt. We're here to protect them, even if that means from themselves."

Arnold shakes his head as he says, "I have no idea what the truth is anymore."

Gordon walks towards Arnold, then hands him a small controller as he says, "Just flick that switch if you ever want to know."

Liang raises his eyebrows as he says, "We wondered how you got that technology. I think it's safe to assume that Henry helped?"

Henry grins as he replies, "Tomorrow, I'll return to my position of actively hunting all Subvert activity, as will Arnold."

Liang's jaw drops as he asks, "How is it the auto-cops did not know who you were when you met Joe?"

Henry grins as he replies, "Some secrets I'll keep to myself, for now anyway."

Gordon stares at the cargo of auto-fixers, then states with urgency, "Aqua needs these now. Let's go!"

The group departs with the cargo transport, leaving Arnold, Liang, and Henry behind.

After a few moments Arnold turns to Henry and says, "I want to know everything."

Henry stares back, then after considering more variables than most could imagine existed, takes a deep breath and then says, "There are no Subverts, no dam, and no power stations." He stares at Arnold as he continues, "We get most of our electricity from Golem One, our water thanks to Aqua, and all we do in return is offer a final option, and a poor one at that, should those facilities fail, or be destroyed."

"Destroyed?" Arnold repeats, "By who?" He asks, suddenly becoming concerned.

"Even after all this time, there are still rogue elements who take what they want by force." Henry stares hard at Arnold, adding, "The last attack on us was repelled by forces from Golem One, but resulted in the loss of our water purification plant, along with causing damage to the outer dome."

Arnold shakes his head as he replies, "If all this is true, why do they help us?"

Henry glances to Liang, stating, "I don't have to tell both of you that this is classified information." Once he is satisfied they both understand the gravity of the situation, he continues, "There are less than two-hundred fifty thousand people left on this continent. Our last contact with anyone else was well over a hundred years ago, when the world's population was around a million."

"What about the rogues you mentioned?" Arnold presses.

"They are the worst!" Henry spits. "We believe they belong to a fleet which roams the ocean. This fleet has limited manufacturing capabilities, and only continues to exist by pilfering what they need

112

from other communities, but in doing so they usually destroy the places they attack."

"That's just plain stupid!" Arnold states, then frowns as he asks, "And that's what happened to us?"

"Pretty much." Henry replies, then adds, "The records indicate that they wanted to siphon off some water, and when they couldn't, they destroyed the facility out of spite."

"I'm surprised they haven't been back." Arnold exclaims.

"Who says they haven't?" Henry questions as he raises his eyebrows, then answering his own question says, "Golem One has stopped many attacks on this place, but in doing so, it has cost them dearly."

"Aqua?" Arnold guesses incorrectly.

"No, no," Henry replies, "many facilities have all fallen over time. Golem One is now all that stands between us and certain death."

"And we all need water!" Arnold states as he nods to where the auto-fixers were, "Which means we need Aqua, even though a fleet of bandits could come swooping down on us at any moment."

"Exactly!" Henry replies.

"I think I'm going to be sick." Arnold states as the ramifications of all he has heard sink in.

Doctor Liang steps forward and says, "Much of this is new to me too." Gazing upward he continues, "Some things I knew, but as for their only being less than a quarter of a million of us left, that was a surprise."

Henry motions to the dome wall as he says, "We've been in contact with other groups like ours, as in they have domes which provide food, water, and energy. Each of us has a common theme of wanting to survive." He takes a deep breath, then flicking his gaze from Liang to Arnold, adds, "Two of these communities were on the opposite side from us when the first war started."

Arnold's jaw drops, while Liang stammers, "And now they're our friends?"

Henry shakes his head as he replies, "Well, yes and no. As I said, we all have a common theme, which includes none of us wanting to restart the war."

Liang shakes his head as he questions, "What was the war over, anyway?"

Henry shakes his head as he gazes upward, "Who knows? Resources, territory?" He shrugs as he says, "Perhaps it was as simple as one side insulting and offending the other? But we'll never know for sure."

Arnold stares at wall where the transport exited, then frowns as he notices where some of the mist from beyond the outer dome has somehow seeped in. The grass is already turning brown where it swirls around malevolently.

With a tremor in his voice, Arnold says, "I hope they succeed."

Chapter Seven - All or Nothing

The scavenging fleet limps away from the devastating explosion. The fact that any of the ships survived the blast from the nuclear stockpile is nothing short of a miracle. The salvage team was to infiltrate the site and commandeer anything of value, instead, they triggered an aging bomb. Luckily, the Commander had ordered all units to move off to a safe distance before the team entered, otherwise all would have been lost.

Fleet Commander Kev sighs as he orders, "Make for Canfield. We require food, and water, along with steel from their dome to repair our damage."

"Yes sir!" Intones the three junior bridge officers.

"And fix those windows!" Kev barks as he storms off the bridge.

The junior officers stare at the shattered glass and wonder how they can possibly replace them. Their supplies of spare window glass ran out years ago, and it is not as if they have any laying around.

Kev is both angry at the dire situation his fleet is in, and yet elated over being alive. When the blast-wave struck, it shattered the windows on the bridge and killed everyone who was above deck. As sheer luck, or fate, would have it, he was below in the head when the blast wave hit. His radiation detector had flashed red as he hurried to the bridge, causing him to stop, and wait. Once it was safe, he returned to the bridge, and took stock of the situation.

The remaining ships limp away, having suffered the loss of eight vessels in the blast, those too small to ride out the ensuing tsunami, leaving fourteen remaining. A far cry from the forty-seven vessels which made up the force when Kev took charge thirty-five years prior, or the two hundred plus which existed at their peak. Most of the ships became unseaworthy and sank from years of neglect; the fleet is over four hundred years old, and time has taken its toll. The fact that any are still afloat amazes all who see the dilapidated hulks. It is no coincidence that the surviving ships are the largest of the original armada. These are the few which have been able to ride out rogue waves, powerful storms, and to stay afloat when compartments unexpectedly flooded.

The flagship is an old aircraft carrier, now converted into a farm ship. Deck after deck is now rice paddies, giving the entire ship a musty smell, and contributing to their rust issues. The next two largest vessels are mighty battleships, their powerful guns long since silenced. Three more are enormous cargo transport vessels, each now used to grow food and to carry their raiding spoils. Another of the flotilla was once a majestic cruise ship, but now it is an ugly mess of patches and repairs. How it remains afloat is a mystery unto itself. Luck has played a major part in this ship's continued endurance, giving the vessel legendary status. Another stroke of luck is the oil tanker which joined them early on after the cataclysm. Its millions of tons of oil being used to keep the engines, and other components, running. However, the ship now rides high in the seas. Its vast holdings, though refilled from time to time, are once more nearly depleted.

The rest of the fleet is a mix-match of surviving military vessels from the long-forgotten wars.

Markings indicating their original allegiances have long since faded from both the ships, and the crew's memories. These vessels had the strongest, and thickest of hulls, made from corrosive resistant composites, along with provisions which saw the original crews through the early holocaust. There is an irony that the nuclear-powered vessels of the day became floating junk yards when their fuel ran out. The older diesel-powered vessels continued on, when they could source fuel. The fluke discovery of an abandoned naval yard on an island, a hundred-seventy years ago, provided the fleet with much needed supplies of oil, fuel, and parts. They stripped the island bare, buying themselves precious time. Since then, raids on settlements have supplemented their provisions. But, each raid provides fewer and fewer provisions for the fleet, causing some of the crew to question how much longer they can last.

These days, crews regularly heave buckets of water overboard from the ship's bilges and other flooded areas, but since the blast-wave, they have been busy night and day, keeping up with the numerous new leaks on all vessels. Bilge pumps remain useless, having seized or broken over the years, with parts for their repair no longer available. Maintaining the ship's engines has always been the fleet's number one priority, with all other considerations being secondary. A ship, dead in the water, is a floating coffin for the crew, and soon stripped of all valuable resources. Some floating hulks have been known to last many years, but all eventually succumb to the ocean. Luckily, the gas which hovers over the water is only damaging to soft membranes, such as a person's lungs and eyes, and has little to no effect on the thick metal of the ships. The gas has thinned over the years, and apart from the occasional dense cloud, now forms a thin layer above the water, like a skin.

Old engines throb, turning ancient propellers, moving the fleet slowly across the calm waters; pushing the ships any faster risks sinking two more of them due to their significant damage. If the seas become rough, these two ships will surely flounder and sink. As it is, the lower decks on these vessels are filling with poisonous gas, hampering efforts to keep the water out.

The carrier is the most important ship in the fleet. It is their last remaining water and fuel conversion ship. Ocean water is drawn inside, from below the surface, in to specialized compartments, where it is filtered and treated. This water is purified for drinking, and used to water the fields, along with everything else such as showers, and cleaning. Some of the water is treated by an electrolysis process, in preparation for becoming fuel for the fleet. The entire system is powered by solar energy, and like everything else, has become unreliable as time marches on. Broken solar panels now outnumber working ones on the carrier's flight deck. The pre-fuel is transferred into specialized storage tanks, where further refinement occurs, prior to being delivered to the fleet's thirsty engines. The process is far from efficient, but it works, and has kept them mobile for centuries. Time is running out for them though; only two of the original eight units remain functional, and they have both suffered recent failures, adding to Kev's stress.

Kev returns to the bridge to find his First Officer standing watch.

"Status?" Kev queries.

"Making best possible speed for the coast near Canfield." He replies.

"Repairs?" Kev demands.

The First Officer sighs, then states, "Two will sink in the next storm, while most of the rest won't last another year or two." He turns to Kev and asks. "Why don't we just see if they'll help us?"

Kev swings a crowbar so fast the officer does not even get a chance to raise his arm in defense. The bar smashes into his skull, cleaving into his brain. The man falls to the ground, bloodied, his body spasms and twitches as he dies.

"I will not be known as the Commander who surrendered the fleet!" Kev curses. He spits on the man as he tosses the bloodied crowbar down.

The junior officers cringe as they attempt to ignore what has just happened.

Kev barks, "Clean that up!" He storms off the bridge, angrier than he has ever been in his life.

The three junior officers are all newly appointed, the others having died in the recent blast. One of them, Freddie, their youngest, cautiously watches as their Commander leaves the bridge, then once he is gone, says, "He's going to get us all killed!"

"That's treason!" Paul states in a hushed tone, not wanting to speak too loudly.

The third, Antonio, looks around the bridge at the broken windows, the blank computer panels which have never worked in his lifetime, and then says, "Do you think Canfield would help us?"

Freddie puts his hands on his hips, then points to the dead officer as he states, "He thought they might."

"Yeah. And look what happened to him!" Paul exclaims fearfully as he motions to the gruesome sight.

Antonio clenches his jaw as picks up the bloodied crowbar, then says, "I'll do it!"

Paul shakes as he stammers, 'What about the rest of the fleet?

Freddie smiles as he replies, "I used to work the fuel cells. If they knew how little we had, or even worse, how tiny an amount we make each day compared to our needs, they'd be happy to have a new Commander."

Antonio nods as he says, "We do spend more time floating about than actually going anywhere!"

Paul frowns as he asks, "But, why would they take us in?"

Antonio points to the other ships as he says, "Between all of us, we're what? Fifteen hundred, hard-working souls?"

Freddie grins as he says, "I hear they have lots of girls!"

Antonio chuckles, "What, you don't like the ones we have here?"

"Well, yeah, but there's not many, not enough for everyone." Freddie replies. He lowers his head as he adds, "Besides, they smell like muskrats."

They all chuckle, not that any of them know what a muskrat is, but anyone who works the rice paddies does get an odd muskiness to their skin. With women being a rare commodity, they work deep inside the ships, performing the safest of tasks, such as maintaining these crops.

Antonio sighs, "You're right. There's not enough girls, and if what I heard is true, Canfield has plenty."

Paul, the ever negative one, retorts, "Where did you hear all this rubbish? And even if it's true, do you think they're going to want you to put your mitts on them." He shakes his head as he adds, "You're dreaming!"

Freddie stares wide-eyed as Kev steps into view and walks toward the bridge. "He's coming!" He hisses skittishly.

Kev steps onto the bridge, looks at the body on the floor and immediately demands, "Why is that…"

He never finishes the sentence. Antonio swings the crowbar down on Kev's head with all the force he can muster. The impact drives Kev to the ground with a resounding squelch.

They all stare transfixed as Kev grunts and attempts to get up, even though his skull is cracked and bleeding. Freddie and Paul stare at Antonio as he swings the bar again, and again, splattering blood everywhere with each juicy thud, until finally, Kev stops moving.

The three of them stare at what they have done, then, as the ramifications of their actions sink in, they become fearful of reprisals. The Commander was popular with many of the crew.

Antonio looks around, then says, "Quick, clean up that blood. We'll toss these bodies overboard at dusk!"

Freddie stares at the blood splattered consoles, walls, floor, and ceiling, then swallows hard as he grabs a rag and begins cleaning. Paul grabs another and helps as Antonio drags the bodies to one side, out of sight to any prying eyes, not that many visit the bridge. Kev's brains smear the ground behind his body, the sight of which causes Freddie to almost throw up. As it is, he dry-heaves as he tries to ignore the grisly skid mark.

As they clean, Antonio stops, then looks sternly at Freddie and Paul and says, "We have not seen either the First Officer or the Commander, and under the fleet charter of ascension, I will assume command!"

Paul frowns as he listens, then his jaw drops as he replies, "Of course!"

Few crew members wander about above decks, especially at nightfall, thus it is relatively easy for the men to carry each body to the side of the bridge, and then drop them into the water. The splash of the bodies goes unnoticed as the fleet plods along. The hours pass as the three continue to stand watch, as if nothing were amiss.

Two junior officers enter the bridge, to begin their duty cycle. It is not unusual for the Commander to be absent, so they think nothing of it.

Antonio turns as the night watch arrives, and with as much sincerity as he can muster asks, "Hey, Smith, have you seen the Commander or the First Officer?"

The newcomers look at each other, shrug, then Smith replies, "Nope, and I can't say it bothers me."

"Well," Antonio replies with a frown, "I think we should search the ship. It's not like them both to be missing, especially all day."

"Yeah… okay." Smith replies hesitantly, then asks, "Shouldn't we wait a bit though? If he's asleep in his cabin, or with someone and we disturb him, we're all in for hell!"

Antonio glances to Freddie and Paul as he runs with the idea, saying, "Yeah, that's what we were thinking too." He then says, "Well, Smith, we'll leave it at your discretion then." With a grin he adds, "Let me know how it goes, will you?"

The two new arrivals nervously glance back and forth, neither wanting the responsibility, then Smith hesitantly says, "But as the current watch, if you think we should, then…" his voice trails off as he leaves the statement hanging.

Inwardly, Antonio sighs in relief; his idea of assuming command is only valid if he is the watch duty officer at the time. Outwardly, he stands emotionless as his mind races. The others think he is simply pausing as he considers what to do.

After a moment, Antonio walks to the ship's speaker system, a series of hollow tubes really. He takes a deep breath then bellows into the largest of them, "Watch Commander Antonio calling Commander Kev to the bridge."

Smith stares in disbelief at Antonio's bravery; no one calls the Commander to the bridge. Nervous sweat builds up as he offers, "Should I go below and start a search?"

Antonio purses his lips together, then says, "Yes, if the Commander is not in his quarters, he may have fallen and be injured."

Paul's eyes flicker to the crowbar, then away quickly as he realizes that they should have removed it from the bridge earlier. Smith does not miss the look though, and spotting the crowbar, he shakes his head as he says, "That's one way to fix the windows. It's bloody cold in here."

Feeling self-conscious at Smith's choice of words, Freddie picks up the crowbar, then says, "The Commander wanted us to replace the windows; figured I'd remove the frames first." He shrugs as he explains, "But we've no replacement glass, so there seems little point."

As soon as the words are out of his mouth, Freddie regrets them. The Commander's orders are always followed, no matter what they are, and yet he clearly failed to comply.

Smith nods as he says, "We'll get to it before Kev, I mean, the Commander, gets here." He points to the broken windows as he asks, "Did you contact the other ships?"

Antonio cringes inwardly, their whole plan is being shot full of holes. This is something else they would have done, if the Commander were alive! He sighs as he replies, "I didn't think it worth the trouble. Last I heard, the fleet was out of glass." He adds, hoping the lie is taken as truth.

"Yeah, I heard that too." Smith quips, trying to sound more knowledgeable than he really is.

The sound of running footfalls reaches their ears, ending their discussion. An older man rushes onto the bridge, and between gasps states, "We can't find the First Officer either! Where could they be?" He asks.

Antonio frowns as he replies, "I have no idea."

"No way Kev fell overboard!" Smith states, "I've seen him stand to a gale force wind!"

"Well, double the search!" Antonio states with conviction. "No, let's get all hands to searching."

Smith shakes his head as he replies, "Can't do that. Half the crew is on water duty."

Antonio's jaw drops as he replies, "It's that bad?"

Smith nods as he adds, "The Commander wouldn't let us stop the fuel cells, which means we're actually sinking."

Freddie, Paul, and Antonio stare at each other in shock. They have been above decks for a long time, and if it were not for the rations stored there, they would have been hungry by now. Antonio cringes once more; if the Commander were alive, they would have never raided the stores. Another mistake!

The night time hours pass slowly as reports continue to arrive that no one has seen either of the missing men. A few described seeing both making their way toward the bridge, but after that, neither had been seen.

As the first rays of sunlight filter onto the bridge, Antonio stands tall, and states, "I will assume command, until such time as either the Commander, or the First Officer are located."

Smith simply shrugs as he replies, "Better you than me. I don't want that crap coming down on me when Kev shows up."

Though exhausted, Antonio feels a sense of relief as he orders, "Halt the fleet and conduct repairs. We'll make for Canfield in two days, where we'll attempt to trade with them."

Smith's eyebrows raise at the unexpected orders. After a brief pause, he replies, "Yes, Commander!"

Antonio feels energized at being referred to as Commander. He smiles as a renewed sense of hope for them all fills his body.

"HEY!" Shouts a voice from outside, "Come look at this!"

Antonio rushes out behind Smith and the others, then looks to where the crewman is pointing. A chill rushes through his body when he notices the blood smear which trails down the side of the ship to the mist covered waters below. He is horrified; obviously, one of the bodies struck the ship when they were tossed over.

Smith stares at the blood then glances at Antonio and frowns. His eyes narrow as he recalls the crowbar, then slowly guesses what happened.

Everyone remains quiet as they all wait for someone to say something. More of the crew arrives, then upon noticing the blood, and the silence, they also remain quiet. A person who goes overboard is considered dead.

After a few nervous moments, Antonio steps forward to speak. Smith unexpectedly cuts him off when he turns toward the crew and shouts, "We all know Commander Kev and the First Officer disagreed about that old weapons facility."

"Aye." Intones the crew in agreement.

Smith glances to Antonio, then continues, "We all know the two argued over it!" He raises his voice as he adds, "Especially after we lost a lot of good sailors!"

"Aye." Responds the crew sullenly.

"Well," Smith states, pointing at the blood, "it looks like they had a fight on the way to the bridge, and both went over."

The crew begins mumbling and muttering amongst themselves; most seem to agree, though a few shake their heads in disbelief.

Smith then points to Antonio, stating, "Commander Antonio Rossi will lead us now."

Antonio's jaw drops; he is speechless.

Smith steps closer to Antonio and mutters, "Told you I didn't want the job!"

Antonio takes a deep breath, then says, "We've lost too many good sailors, and our ships are all but rusted away."

The crew reluctantly agrees, though some voice their confidence in the ships, as if they will somehow continue on for an eternity.

Antonio nods as he continues, "These are grand ships, but it is time to throw our lot in with a larger group; for all our sakes."

"Commander Kev would have none of that!"
Shouts a crewman angrily.

Smith barks back, "Tell that to the dead!"

Antonio points to the man, then orders, "Any man, or woman, who wishes to remain at sea, follow that man. I will leave you enough ships, including this one, if that's your choice."

The man strides closer, then puffs out his chest as he boasts, "All will follow me!"

Smith, being a junior officer, knows more about the fleet's status than most of the crew. He boldly steps in front of the boisterous man, and with a wide grin states, "All who follow you to the sea, will die by the sea."

Antonio nods to the gathering crew as he asks, "How many of you does it take to stop us sinking?" Before anyone can answer, he shouts, "Half of you! And this is the best ship in the fleet."

Many of the crew who were standing with the vocal crewman, step away. Another calls out, "Commander, what are your orders?"

Antonio puts his hands on his hips as he replies, "We sail for the coast, where I'll go ashore and negotiate our terms with Canfield." He pauses for a moment, then continues, "Should I fail to return, do as you wish, but should I be successful, we will have a new place to call 'home', a place with fresh food and water!"

Most of the crew cheers. Food is scarce, and although they have water, it is rationed, and at times has a strange taste. Those who do not celebrate the idea, do so out of fear of change, they only know their lives at sea.

The man who confronted Antonio glances around warily as his supporters fade away.

Antonio points to the man and demands, "Crewman! Your name?"

"Marco," he replies as his confidence dwindles further.

"Crewman Marco," Antonio retorts, "you challenge me again, it's mutiny!"

"Understood Commander." Marco replies sullenly. He quickly defends himself, "I was just looking out for the lads."

Antonio considers the crew's respect for the man, then says, "If you're looking out for them, then come ashore with me."

The crew cheers at the idea, causing Marco to stop in his tracks; the idea of going ashore terrifies him. He hates shore missions, but not because of the danger. The land just feels wrong; it does not move.

Smith seizes the opportunity to further unite the crew, "Call all ships. Tell them to ready the landing craft. Our new Commander has a mission where he is the one going and risking his life, and not sending others to do his dirty work!"

The crew cheers loudly, celebrating. Kev was respected for his seamanship, but when it came to shore patrols, he never did put his boots on the ground, or risk his own life when it came to sealing sections of the ship off.

Antonio nods to Smith and says, "Thanks, that was well done!"

Smith hold his hand out, then while shaking hands, he stares into Antonio's eyes and vows, "I will serve you well, Commander!"

Antonio glances to Freddie and Paul, then states, "We're going to make a great team."

Smith grins, "I think you're mad going ashore, but then, I see your point. Our ships have just about had it."

Antonio sighs as he quietly mutters, "I just hope they help us!"

Golem One

Dianne watches three craft as they surge along the water, then land on the beach. Two of them stop, and ominously wait on the sand. Water, rubbish, and mist, lapping at their flanks, heavy guns protruding from all sides. Oddly, the unarmed one presses forward. She frowns, deeply concerned by their arrival, especially at this time.

Jerry stares through binoculars at the craft, then swings his attention to the fleet which is anchored off shore. They have been monitoring the approaching armada for an entire day, from the moment they appeared on the horizon. He can see where some of the ships are so badly damaged, water and mist seeps inside them, with people tossing bucket after bucket of water overboard in a clearly desperate move to keep the ships afloat.

Dianne considers her options as she taps the windowsill. She sighs as she asks, "Is that a new force? It's too small to be the raiding fleet we've seen before."

"I don't know, but it looks like they're heading for Canfield." Jerry states, quickly adding, "But if you want me to intercept that transport before we lose it in the mist, I'll have to go now."

Dianne frowns at the odd situation. Historically, the pirates landed in force, in the dark, raided, then quickly retreated, affording them little time to react. This time they have landed during the day, in small numbers, and are moving slowly.

Jerry whispers into his communicator, quietly issuing instructions as he paces back and forth, impatiently waiting.

Dianne's eyes narrow as she says, "Their presence will hinder our repair efforts of Aqua. I got word this morning that our engineers figured out how to use the auto-fixers." She sighs as she adds, "So, I had planned to send two of them with the repair crews today."

"We haven't fully evacuated the facility either. We're having trouble encouraging the fish to leave." Jerry replies, shaking his head. His tone picks up as he adds, "But, our latest reports indicate that the fish are attracted to those ship's engines."

Dianne fingers drum on the windowsill, tapping as she ponders what to do. Sighing, she adds, "Yes, but then they practically parked over Aqua, which I have trouble believing is a coincidence."

"They haven't attacked." Jerry ventures, positively.

"Stop that landing craft!" Dianne orders. She drops her fist on the window ledge, adding vehemently, "Bring them here. We need to know what they're up to."

"Yes ma'am!" Jerry replies as he hurries to the elevator.

The vehicle Jerry and his two colleagues uses, is different than the one Miranda controlled, in that it has a large double-barreled machine gun mounted on the roof. The vehicle's wheels squeal as Jerry accelerates out of the cave, its engine pushed to its limit. He had ordered the vehicle, and his crew to be ready, just in case.

The three-man team remains vigilant as they leave the high road, keeping out of sight of the pirate craft on the shore. Jerry slows as they drop down into a gully, entering the thick mist. The uneven terrain forces Jerry to slow down even more, but they are still bounced around as he presses on.

Jerry scowls, "We lost 'em!"

"They're heading for Canfield! Right?" States one of his men.

"I know," Jerry sighs, then adds, "I just didn't want to confront them in the mist, that's all."

Meanwhile, in the other ground craft, Antonio stares at the mist warily. He turns to Marco, and says, "I'm going to guess that's even more poisonous than the fog banks we see from time to time."

"Aye." Marco replies shakily. His hands grip his controls firmly as he moves them over the rough terrain. His voice wavers as he asks, "How do you plan to contact them?"

Antonio stares at the controls blankly, then replies, "All we can hope for is that they pick up our transmission." He is still trying to figure out what does what, he has never been on a transport before.

Both vehicles travel through the thick fog, with one or the other occasionally emerging out of the mist as they follow the rise and fall of the land. Far off, in Golem One's tower, Dianne watches anxiously as each vehicle briefly appears, but never both at the same time. They are getting closer and closer together however.

"Oh crap!" Jerry exclaims as he slams on the brakes, rocking them back and forth on their suspension.

Marco swerves as he too stops as quickly as he can. The other transport is a complete surprise to the two of them. His face twitches as he glances to Antonio.

The two vehicles avoid colliding by the narrowest of margins, with both coming to rest with a hand space between them.

Antonio and Marco stare wide-eyed into the barrels of a machine gun which swivels their way at the same time their speakers crackle, "Pirates! Remain where you are."

"We found them!" Exclaims one of Jerry's colleagues, stating the obvious, as he wipes sweat from his brow.

Jerry nods as he broadcasts, "I am unclear of your intent. Follow us to our base, or I will open you up to the gas."

Antonio glances to Marco then reluctantly asks, "How do we respond?"

Marco snorts, "I bet you're glad you brought me along now. He shakes his head as he points to a switch, instructing, "Flip that up to talk, and down to stop."

Antonio stares through the thick swirling fog at the machine gun which squarely points at them. He takes a deep breath, then replies as confidently as he can, "The old Fleet Commander is dead. As the new Fleet Commander, I wish to discuss terms with Canfield."

Marco's face twitches again; the idea of surrendering sends chills up his back. He toys with the idea of killing Antonio, then returning to claim the fleet. But he is smart enough to realize that the crew needs a safe haven, so he reluctantly complies.

Jerry frowns as he silently mouths to his colleagues, "Terms?"

When there is no immediate reply, Antonio becomes anxious. Seeing Marco's reaction, it dawns on him how his words could be interpreted.

He immediately adds, "We're not surrendering! My crew is hard working and deserves equal standing with your people."

Jerry scowls as he ponders the situation. He hates politics; that is why he is a front-line soldier. He considers his own words carefully, then replies, "We have defended ourselves from you and your kind for many years, and now you wish to join us? That's for my leaders to decide. So, as I said before, follow me or die!"

Antonio looks at Marco, then shrugs as he replies, "We'll follow, but if you think you can parlay us for terms, that won't happen."

Jerry stares at the other craft perplexed. He has no idea what they are talking about and does not reply. Instead he lifts his finger and swirls it around, indicating for them to get moving.

Marco follows the other craft as it moves off, his eyes locked on the barrels of the gun which never wavers from them. He glances to Antonio, then upon his nod, sends a brief pre-planned coded communication to the other transports, indicating that they have made contact. The simple squawk picked up by Jerry and Golem One, means nothing to them.

A large contingent of heavily armed guards awaits the transports as they enter the underground cavern. Antonio and Marco have never seen such defenses as those which line the walls on the way in and are further stunned by the sheer firepower which confronts them in the cavern.

Antonio frowns as he turns to Marco and says, "I don't think we're the only threat these people have had to face."

Marco agrees, "For sure!" Then with a deepening frown, questions, "We've sailed the oceans for centuries, and I've never seen a force that could beat this. So, who are they defending themselves against?"

"That's something we need to know." Antonio replies.

Marco turns to Antonio as a chill runs up his spine. His jaw drops as he says, "There are other fleets! I swear Kev used to communicate with them. I always thought he was talking with our ships. But if they were all working together, then…" his voice trails off; he is lost for words.

Antonio replies, "That would make a lot of sense. It would also explain how we always seemed to just have enough to get by, but never too much. Perhaps we've been trading our surplus with others."

Marco scowls, "It's a pity the whole command crew were killed in the blast, and then we lost our Commander, and First Officer."

"Someone has to know about the other fleets. We'll ask the other ship captains when we get back." Antonio replies. He wonders how such a secret could have been kept from the crew. He considers the many times they found supplies. and wonders about their own stocks.

Marco points outside, interrupting Antonio's thoughts as he says, "I guess it's time to find out if we're prisoners, or guests!"

Antonio nods, then replies, "Well, let's open the door, and find out."

Dianne approaches the group, then stops as Jerry lifts a hand. He rarely stops her, but this time he is being extremely cautious.

Jerry waves his gun toward the two pirates as they step out, demanding, "Keep your hands where I can see 'em!"

Antonio lifts his hands, then walks slowly toward Jerry, where he stops and says, "You can see our fleet, and our heavy guns. If we wanted to destroy Canfield, we would have done so already!"

Jerry doubts the massive guns he saw on the ships work, but he has seen stranger things. He glances to Dianne, then introduces her, "This is Dianne; she runs things around here."

Antonio nods, then motions as he replies, "This is my friend Marco, while I'm Antonio, the Fleet Commander."

Dianne strides forward, her eyes narrow as she declares, "No Fleet Commander would ever dare walk into this place."

"Why not?" Antonio replies gruffly.

Jerry glances back and forth, then interjects, "Commander, you need to understand this; whenever we see your kind, you're killing, stealing, or destroying."

"You don't know my kind." Antonio retorts. "You have all this land, and yet look at you. You stay in this one little area."

"Where else would we go?" Dianne replies, taking over the conversation once more.

Even though Antonio and Marco have spent their entire lives on the flagship, both know of islands where trees flourish, and places where even a few small animals eke out an existence. The only people they know of, however, live in domes, like Canfield's, or in underground bunkers, like the one they are in.

Marco cast his gaze at the dozens of armed men, then offers, "Look, I'm not saying its easy out there, but if you guys explored a little, you would see that the whole world isn't like this."

Dianne places her hands on her hips as she demands, "Then why are you here?"

Antonio sighs, "The only survivors, are people like you and me. Those able to grow food, purify water, and either get above the gas, or block it out."

Dianne stops at his words, 'you and me', then after hesitating, asks, "Why did you come here?"

"We weren't coming here." Antonio replies indignantly, "We were heading to Canfield."

"But why?" Dianne presses.

"We wish to join them!" Antonio replies with a smile, then adds, "We have fifteen hundred hard working men and women."

Jerry snorts, "But if we should be out 'exploring', why is it you want to go and lock yourselves inside a dome?"

Marco's face twitches as he listens to the way the talks are going; they are not going well.

Antonio lowers his gaze as he replies, "Our ships are too badly damaged to sail the oceans anymore. We have no choice really."

Dianne's eyes narrow as she presses, "How have you lived all this time? Raiding others to survive!" She spits.

"No! No!" Antonio responds, shocked, then admits, "Well, we have raided places here and there. But," he adds with mounting pride, "we also grow our own food, filter our own water, and even process our own fuel!"

Gordon, who has been hanging back, listening, suddenly gasps, "I have an idea!"

Everyone turns to look at Gordon, surprised by his outburst.

Dianne lifts her eyebrows as she says, "Please, share your epiphany?"

Gordon grins as he says, "It's so damn simple!" Then upon seeing all the blank faces, says, "We use the auto-fixers to repair the fleet, Aqua, the dome, then we ALL look for a new place to call home."

"You can repair our ships?" Antonio replies, doubtingly.

"Sure, why not," Gordon says, "it's just hull plating, and from what I understand, we manufacture steel right here in Golem One."

Antonio reluctantly admits, "We're down to two fuel cells, and they don't produce near enough fuel for the fleet."

"I am sure we can repair them too!" Gordon replies positively. He thumps his fist into his palm, adding, "I bet Henry can you get what you need."

Jerry stares at Antonio, then glances at Dianne, before stating, "How can we trust you?"

Antonio takes a deep breath, then looking to Marco nods as he replies, "I can't answer that." He shifts his gaze to Dianne, then says, "You only have my word, and as far as you know, it's not worth a damn."

Marco shifts uncomfortably, then says, "He's our Fleet Commander, and he came here, unarmed. That's gotta count for something?"

Gordon walks though the ring of guards as he says, "I've spent my entire life reading people."

Everyone is quiet as Gordon stops in front of Antonio. No one knows quite which way this is going to go as both men stare at each other.

A few tense moments pass, then Gordon extends a hand as he offers, "I trust you! You have honest lines."

Antonio is unsure what honest lines are, but takes the offered hand firmly and shakes.

Dianne puts a hand to her lips as she ponders what to do. She motions for Jerry to lower his weapon, which as he does, so do the rest of the guards. The tension in the area immediately drops, though the handful of hidden snipers arranged around the walls remain vigilant.

Dianne puts her hands together as she speaks, "I will contact the council, and seek their advice. But for now, let's get Aqua, AND the ships repaired. That's my good faith offering." She glances to Gordon, and hopes he is right, otherwise people will die, good people.

Gordon grins as he says, "Pete can take us to Canfield, where we can get Henry's help."

Miranda and Joe groan; what he means, is that the two of them will go too. Pete shakes his head, it seems he is their designated driver, again!

Antonio offers, "I'll take anyone who wants to go, and give them a tour of the flagship."

Dianne nods as she replies, "Joe will go with you. He can get a list of your needs, and then you can all meet at Canfield, and relay your requirements to Gordon and Henry. In the meantime, we do have a limited number of steel plates we could let you have. If we're going to be friends, it has to start somewhere."

Joe stares at Miranda, stunned. He was not looking forward to a trip to Canfield, and now she wants him to visit a pirate fleet! He glances to Maggie, who is making her way to Dianne's side, then upon seeing her beaming smile, he grins too. He watches as Maggie gets on her tip-toes and while looking at him, whispers into Dianne's ear. He has no idea what she is saying, but Dianne flicks her gaze Joe's way, then seems to blush.

Dianne immediately swats at Maggie, then turns her attention to Antonio. She takes a deep breath, then says, "Antonio, let's help each other, we could use some manpower in the foundries."

Antonio lowers his gaze as he replies, "Most of the crew spends their time keeping the ships afloat. None of them have functioning bilge pumps anymore."

"Pumps are something of a priority to us," Dianne replies, "but, I'm sure we can spare a few."

Marco's jaw drops as he blurts out, "You'd give us pumps?"

Dianne nods as she replies, "We have to start somewhere, don't we?"

"But pumps?" Marco stammers, "That's a lot!"

"Not for us," Dianne replies, adding, "you'd be surprised by what we can do."

Antonio casts his gaze around, then says, "Okay. You're willing to give us pumps, and steel to repair our leaking hulls, and all you want is people to help?"

Marco quietly mumbles, "It sounds like they want some of our crew here, as leverage."

Antonio grins as he replies without moving his lips, "Can't blame them."

Dianne stares hard at Antonio, then says, "Come with me."

Everyone watches as Dianne walks toward the elevator. Antonio takes a nervous breath, then motions for Marco to stay as he follows. Jerry joins them, as does Joe, although his only invitation was a smile and giggle from Maggie. They silently ride to the top of the tower, where Antonio steps into the control room. He is immediately awed by what he sees. Functioning computers, along with a majestic view.

Dianne glances to Jerry, then says, "Show him!"

Jerry had not expected that they would ever show outsiders their long-range defense system, but he understands her reasoning. His face is a stern mask as he motions for Antonio to look through a fixed set of large binoculars.

Antonio expects to see his fleet, but as he looks he does not expect to see a red crosshair aimed squarely at the carrier. He turns to Jerry and shrugs as he says, "Yes, you can see the fleet. So?"

Jerry pauses for a moment, then says, "The crosshair you saw, it's attached to our targeting systems."

"I expect nothing less," Antonio replies more bravely than he feels.

Dianne shakes her head as she says, "You don't understand. After the last raid on Canfield, the one where the attackers damaged the outer dome, we decided to unseal our remaining nuclear weapons."

Antonio stares at Dianne blankly as he repeats, "Nuclear weapons!"

"Yes, we still have a few long-range missiles, which we have kept maintained, just in case..." She lets the words trail off.

"But, you didn't use them." Antonio replies cautiously, then says, "I for one, am glad you didn't, but why not?"

"I was curious as to why you would approach slowly, and during the daylight, knowing you could be tracked." She replies.

Antonio shrugs, "To be honest, I thought Canfield defended itself. I had no idea this place existed at all." It then dawns on him as to why the facility is so well defended; it is one of the last of the old war-fortresses. He has only heard stories about them and thought the stories to simply be fairytales.

Jerry nods to the fleet, then says, "How many more of your kind are out there?"

"I have no idea." Antonio replies, then with a sigh continues, "There was a nuclear blast from a depot we were raiding. I'm sure you saw it!" He exclaims, interrupting himself.

"Oh, we saw it." Dianne replies, her eyes blazing into Antonio's.

"Well," Antonio presses on as he avoids her intense scrutiny, "that blast killed the flagship's command crew, and pretty much everyone who was above decks, which means that many of our ships lost their captains."

"Okay," Dianne queries, "and?"

"Marco and I think there are other fleets, but we don't know for sure. You see, I took over the fleet after the blast, before which I was on flood-watch duty."

Jerry sighs, "Get to the point, will you!"

Antonio glances back and forth, then says, "Anything they knew, died with them. They left no notes, no maps, no clues about other fleets. Nothing!"

Dianne puts a hand to her forehead where a headache is forming. She cringes as she states, "So you really don't know." She narrows her eyes as she asks, "But, if your fleet were repaired, could you convince others to join you?"

"I wish I could tell you what you want to hear. But in truth, I'm as scared of other fleets as you are."

Chapter Eight - Unity

Henry has to read the message twice before its ramifications sink in. He leans back in his chair and closes his eyes as he figures out how these new developments will impact his plan. With a sigh he realizes that he is a hypocrite. He wanted Gordon and Miranda to see what life was like outside the dome, while he remained safe and insulated.

He reads key words from the message once more, '…meeting of all community leaders…'

Staring at his ceiling, he mumbles, "With a fleet, we can do so much more! But how to get the fleet?" He taps his fingers on his armrests as ideas race through his head.

Sighing, it dawns on him what must be done. The builders of the dome knew this day would come, and now it falls on his shoulders to tell the inhabitants the truth. A chill runs up his spine as he realizes just how high the stakes have become. If he tells the inhabitants about the world, and the fleet sails away, the people will lose all hope. It all rests in Joe's hands now, perhaps even the fate of humanity, for without that fleet, they have no way of travelling to new lands.

The Fleet

Sitting behind Antonio and Marco, Joe tries to smile as the transport bobs up and down in the ocean swell. The motion of the waves makes him a little queasy, unlike his last trek into the water. Two other craft follow, each carrying a sizable cargo of steel plates which have been treated for ocean use, and underwater welding units, along with specialized heavy-duty wetsuits.

Golem One is preparing another transport, which will make its way out to the fleet, once Joe safely returns. This load consists of a dozen pumps, along with technicians who know how to install them. Meanwhile, repair crews for Aqua anxiously await the outcome of Joe's visit to the fleet, before they too depart.

Joe recalls his 'mission brief', and suddenly feels as if the weight of the world were on his shoulders. If he knew that it was true, that the fate of hundreds of thousands counted on him, he would probably have a nervous breakdown. He never thought of himself as an ambassador, and yet here he is; representing Canfield, Golem One, Aqua, and unbeknownst to him, other communities on the continent.

The fleet looms ahead, getting larger and larger as they approach. The vessels seem too huge to be floating on the water, especially the flagship with its flat top, as well as the two warships with their enormous guns pointing landward.

Joe's jaw drops when he notices the patchwork cruise liner; how it still floats baffles him. He cranes his head upward as they approach a wall of steel, its sides pitted and dented from centuries at sea.

He frowns when he sees the vast number of repaired sections, mostly along the misty waterline, and wonders how they fixed that with the deadly gas. He is stunned when he realizes that many of the repairs seem to have been conducted from the inside. The more he looks, the more concerned he becomes. Vast sections of the hull are peeling apart; the internal repairs obviously inadequate, and temporary. Some of the jagged holes are large enough to allow him to see inside.

The transports enter an open section in the rear of the carrier, where aging doors close behind them. They drive up eroded ramps, then once well clear of the gas, stop.

Antonio turns to Joe and says, "Welcome to the fleet."

"Thank you." He replies nervously.

Marco slaps Joe on the back as he says, "C'mon, we're not that bad!"

It takes a few minutes for Joe's eyes adjust to the dim interior. Looking around he sees almost as much light is filtering in through the numerous holes in the hull, as is provided by the dim lights overhead. The first thing he notices about the crew is how pale and sickly they look; much worse than Antonio or Marco. Their skin appears leathery while their eyes are red tinged, as if irritated. He is about to wipe his own stinging eyes when Marco stops him.

"Don't do that down here," Marco instructs, "you'll just make it worse."

Antonio nods as he says, "It's better on the upper decks, let's go!"

Joe feels self-conscious as he walks past the crew; compared to them, he is overweight, and soft. Lowering his head, humbled, he walks on. He follows Antonio up a series of metal rung steps, then stops and looks down at the forty or so people below. They are obviously excited about the steel plates and unload them enthusiastically.

As Joe watches, he suddenly feels inspired. He lifts his fist in the air as he calls out, "I have only recently discovered the real world, and in that short time have met three new communities, all hard-working communities. One on land, another below the waves, and now you people of the sea!"

Those working below stop what they are doing and look up.

Joe feels a confidence he has never experienced before, and then with all eyes on him, says, "I can only image what the future holds, if we can all work together!"

The crew cheers loudly.

Antonio turns to Marco and nods as a smile expands across his face. Those few words were the hope they all wanted. Joe's tour of the carrier consists of walking along dim corridors, lit in places only by slits in the hull. They walk past musty rice paddies, storage areas with lots of open space, and then, judging by the noises emanating from one area, they pass the engine room.

Antonio turns to Joe and says, "Okay, enough of this. Let me show you the bridge."

They climb stairwell, upon stairwell, until finally arriving at the bridge, where two other men are standing watch.

Antonio motions to the two as he introduces them, "Officers, Freddie, and Paul. Between the four of us," He nods to Marco, "we run everything."

Joe smiles, "I am Joe, from Canfield."

Antonio relays the news of the trip ashore, while Joe gawks at the view. From this vantage point he can see the entire fleet, as well as the hills where Golem One rests. Surprisingly he can even discern the top of a distant dome, one he correctly assumes is Canfield. He suddenly realizes that all he has to do is to manage the situation as though he were managing a new stock market client. He needs a hard sell, where the client is presented with nothing but a win-win scenario.

Turning to Antonio, Joe says, "I can't believe you've survived all this time on the water."

Antonio nods as he replies, "Our previous commanders raided communities such as yours, for supplies, but no longer." He glances to Marco as he continues, "If we are to survive, then we must find another way."

"Here, here." Marco agrees.

Joe has been waiting for an opportunity to present Dianne's idea, and can think of no better time than now. He takes a deep breath, then looking at Antonio states, "If we could join forces, then perhaps we could repair the ships and sail the seas in search of a new home."

"We had thought the fleet to be a lost cause." Antonio glances to Marco as he continues, "But, I can see that if we work together, we could do a lot better than wait until our ships sink."

Marco adds his thoughts, "It should be easy enough to convince the captains that this is the best way." He presses, "Especially if they get to keep their ships!"

Joe grins as he replies, "Dianne is committed to saving the fleet."

Antonio frowns as he says, "She just wants to use the fleet you mean."

"Yes, and no." Joe replies hesitantly, then explains, "You'd still be the Fleet Commander, but

147

once the fleet becomes part of the greater community, you would go where the ruling body thinks best."

Marco snorts, "Like we'd be taking orders!"

Joe holds his hand up as he explains, "Antonio, as the Fleet Commander, you'd have a voice on the Council."

Antonio's jaw drops as he repeats, "Council! I'd be a part of your Council?"

Joe nods as he says, "The Council will have nine seats, with all decisions requiring a majority vote."

Marco narrows his eyes as he interrupts, "The captains have to agree, before we get to that point."

Antonio walks to the open windows on the bridge, then casts his gaze over the fleet as he considers their future. A few moments pass before he orders, "Get the captains together. I'll get their thoughts on this matter, before making a decision."

"Aye, Commander!" Marco replies, then leaves the bridge.

Antonio turns to Joe and says, "Go with Marco, while I talk with the captains."

"Okay." Joe replies, then hurries after the departing man.

Marco stops then nods to Joe as he approaches, then both continue toward the signal room.

Antonio has decided to join forces with the land-based groups, and although a part of him dislikes the idea, he is excited at the prospect of being able to sail the seas with ships that have a place to repair. He will put a word in the captains' ears about fresh food, fuel, along with other supplies, adding that they will be able to keep their ships, their repaired ships!

The signal room is a small area, from which Marco uses a light to flash a message to the fleet. Each ship, in return, flashes an acknowledgement. A few minutes pass before they signal again, with each ship captain confirming they are on their way. The fleet begins moving closer to the flagship as transports leave the carrier, to pick up the captains from each of the surviving ships.

Marco is not sure what to do with Joe while they wait, then decides, "C'mon, I'll show you more of the ship."

"Sounds good." Joe replies, curious about what else there is to see.

Joe follows Marco, meeting crew men and women and visiting areas he had no idea existed. He thought Antonio's tour was all encompassing and is surprised by the vastness of the carrier.

The number of rice fields that exist is a shock; level upon level, and section after section is filled with them. They seem to be everywhere. Long gashes in the hull provide some light, complimenting the glow from huge tubes which are suspended overhead. He wonders where they get replacement tubes from, then recalls Antonio's comments about the fleet raiding communities for what they needed.

Moving on, they head aft, and down, until they arrive at the engine room.

Marco stops, then points inside, proudly proclaiming, "We kept 'em running!" He grins as he motions for Joe to go inside.

Stepping into the room, Joe's nose is instantly assaulted by the smell of burning oil, steam, and unwashed bodies. He almost gags as he tries to comprehend what it is he is looking at. A filthy man hovers over one of the engines, seemingly possessed as he pours a mix of black liquid over some parts, wipes others down, and then leans in to listen.

A dozen or so others mill about, each taking care of one piece of equipment or another. Pipes crisscross the area as if they were out of control vines, with many obviously not being where originally intended.

Walking carefully, Joe steps over hot pipes, dodges sizzling water drops, and keeps clear of pools of oil as he explores. Looking at the walls, he can see where, once, each engine had its own compartment, but now, six exist in one vast area, supported by huge steel girders. Some of the men acknowledge him with a smile, but the majority simply scowl, as if he were intruding on their private domain.

Marco slaps him on the back as he laughs. Raising his voice, to be heard over the din, he says, "I bet you've never seen engines like those."

"To be honest, I have no idea what all this is." Joe admits. He gazes in wonder at the room, and the men in it. The only engines he knows of are electric motors.

"They get loud when they're running hard, but right now they're idling," Marco explains, "just in case we have to get out of here in a hurry." Inwardly he is cringing at Antonio's order; the fleet is using fuel faster than it can be replenished.

Pointing at a man whose head rests near an engine, Joe fires off a series of questions, "Why would he do that? I can hear the engines from here! Won't he go deaf?"

Marco grins as he explains, "They're the lifers. Each one is responsible for his own engine."

Joe shakes his head as he replies despondently, "What a horrible life!"

"No, no." Marco quips back, "They get the best food, water, and if they call for anything, and I mean anything! They get it." He takes a deep breath, then points down to one of the men as he proudly states, "That's my boy! Eric. Engine six."

Joe jumps as a squeal of releasing steam fills the air. He points to a group of men near the offending boiler as he asks, "Do they look after those…" His voice trails off; he is not sure what they are.

"Yeah. Each engine had two boilers, but over time, they had to make changes, to keep everything running."

The room suddenly makes sense to Joe. He nods as he points, "So, if I've got this right, those three engines are off, as are the boilers behind them, and it looks like two of the engines have been stripped down for parts."

"Yeah," Marco replies, "I probably shouldn't tell you this, but engine five has just about had it."

"I can't believe you kept them going all this time!" Joe exclaims.

"We got lucky when we found that abandoned naval base." Marco frowns as he adds, "If what they say is true, the Fleet Commander of the time repaired the entire fleet. But then, that was before my grandfather's time."

"Why don't you go back?" Joe asks, confused, "Surely there must still be stuff left!"

Marco slowly rolls his tongue around his mouth before admitting, "We don't know where it is."

Joe scratches his head as something else which is bothering him comes to mind, "Hey, where do you get all the fuel? Engines that big have to use a lot!"

Marco considers what to share, then deciding that he trusts the man, replies, "We have enough to sail for three days at top speed. Ah, well, our top speed is around five to six knots now." He lifts his finger as he adds, "But! If we move at one to two knots, we have maneuvering fuel for a month."

"A month!" Joe exclaims, then recalling the fuel cells, asks, "How much can you make?"

Marco sighs as he replies, "Well, I am not good at figuring that out, but the lads reckon that for every day we idle, it's two days of dead time."

"How do…" Joe stops talking as Marco waves his hand in the air and shakes his head.

"If you want to know more, you'll have to ask Antonio."

Joe has so many questions but understands and keeps quiet. He nods in agreement, then follows Marco, leaving the massive engines behind.

Marco scratches his chin as he ponders what to show Joe. His eyes light up as he asks, "You ever see a plane?"

Joe recalls the one at the airport, with its broken wing, then replies, "I've seen one, but it was a ruined mess."

"Well, we kept one, for show you know." Marco states as he hurries off.

Joe picks up his pace and is surprised when he is taken to the forward section of the carrier. His ears are still ringing from the engine room as he diligently follows Marco. Antonio had pointed in the direction they are going and had said that it was all fields and crops. The pair climb numerous stairwells, until coming to the level below the flight deck.

Marco chatters as they continue on, "We're going to the original maintenance area for the planes. The elevator that moves them from below decks jammed, with the last one stuck on it. We couldn't move it, and there's no sense stripping it down for parts, so the lads have been keeping it clean."

Arriving at the platform, Joe is stunned by the sight. A gleaming fighter plane rests atop an elevator. Its clear canopy reflects the dim glow from the lights above; its swept back wings and tail fins still carry their original grey paint along with strange symbols. The deck overhead is sealed shut, protecting the plane from the elements.

Marco points at the plane as he explains, "The crew gets bored, so they have kept it clean all these years. It's become something of a symbol to the lads." He nods as he purses his lips, adding, "It represents hope."

A series of catwalks have been built that lead to the elevator, while at some point in the past, a railing was built around edges to stop people from falling off.

"Go on," Marco urges as Joe glances to him, "take a look."

Joe steps closer, then peering through the canopy is surprised to see the interior in all its glory. The controls and seat are aged, but still appear to be in great condition. He walks around the plane, careful not to fall off the platform. Looking under the plane, the only sign as to its true condition is its flat and decayed tires.

Marco grins as he boasts, "This ship had lots of those!"

"Where did they all go?" Joe asks, curiosity getting the better of him.

Marco shakes his head, "No one knows."

Joe points to the symbols as he asks, "What do they mean?"

Marco grins as he replies, "You haven't noticed? The same symbols are all over. It's the side this ship was originally fighting for."

Joe's jaw drops as he recalls the remnants of the symbols he had walked passed. He frowns as he asks, "A whole fleet that survived?"

"Well, not really." Marco replies slowly, then after scratching his head, he continues, "The story goes, that after the 'Big One', whatever that was, the fleet captains from all over got together. They decided on a Commander, then went looking for resources, and survivors."

"Wow!"

"Not all the captains agreed though!" Marco continues even slower, "The others went off to become pirate fleets."

"I thought you were the pirates?" Joe blurts out before thinking.

"Aye," Marco replies sullenly, "We've done that too, when we had to."

Joe lifts his head up as a chill works its way up his spine. He swallows hard as he says, "If you're not the pirate fleet, then they're still out there. We have to warn the others."

Marco shrugs as he replies indifferently, "They stay away from us, and we stay away from them. Besides, it's been a long while since I last laid eyes on 'em."

Turning his attention back to the plane, Joe walks around and around it in awe, but his thoughts are on warning Dianne.

The Gathering

The debate had raged about where to meet, when Miranda had surprised them all with her suggestion. While repairs get underway on Aqua, thanks to the fleet drawing the massive sea creatures away, an unlikely group of people meets.

Henry stands in the doorway to Resort Fiesta, with Joe fidgeting nervously on his right, waiting. Gordon and Miranda are already inside, preparing the meeting room, along with the other amenities. Most of Fiesta's employees were given the day off, and all visitations cancelled, leaving the entire facility at their disposal.

Pete drives his transport to the front door, then stops, allowing his passengers to disembark.

Joe smiles as he announces, "This is Dianne and Jerry, of Golem One, along with Ken, who is representing Aqua."

Henry greets them with an outstretched hand as he says, "Welcome to Resort Fiesta."

Dianne smiles as she shakes Henry's hand, saying, "Thank you for providing a venue for our meeting."

Jerry's large rifle appears to be casually slung over his shoulder, but he is well practiced in its use, and could easily bring it to bear.

Another familiar vehicle arrives, its sides pitted from years of corrosion.

Joe grins as he announces, "Fleet Commander Antonio, and his associate Marco." He nods to both respectfully, then looks past them. A light glinting off a distant vehicle catches his attention.

Henry shakes Antonio's hand then Marco's as he repeats, "Welcome to Resort Fiesta."

Marco glances to Jerry, then cringes as he realizes that his side-arm is no match for the weapon on the man's back.

The shiny personal transit vehicle arrives, then as all eyes turn to it, two men step out.

Joe smiles as he recognizes the pair. He clears his throat, getting everyone's attention as he announces, "Doctor Liang and Detective Arnold."

Henry grins as he corrects Joe, "Senior Lead Investigator Arnold, Doctor Liang, thank you for joining us at this historic meeting."

Miranda walks through the foyer to the group as she offers, "Fiesta's spa facilities are at your disposal."

Marco mumbles, "We spend our entire lives on the ocean, and she offers us a bath!"

Antonio nudges him with his elbow as he quietly retorts, "True, but I for one wouldn't want to bathe in the seas!"

"Aye, "Marco begrudgingly agrees, then presses, "but still, water?"

"Water!" Joe blurts. "Does that mean...?" He begins to ask before realizing the company he is in and stops.

Miranda nods as she answers his unfinished question, "The auto-fixers completed repairs to the pipework this morning and are now working on the domes."

Henry speaks in a loud, yet polite tone, "I think we would all benefit from a spa and massage, followed by a fine meal, before we sit down to discuss our future."

Three hours later they all meet in the dining hall, each of them refreshed, and relaxed. Jerry and Marco eye each other for a while, but once they realize that hostilities are unlikely, they sit with each other and talk. As the meals are served, the pair shows each other their weapons, with Jerry's large rifle clearly being the superior firearm.

Once the dinner service is complete, Henry stands and raises his glass as he says, "I think it's time for proper introductions." He casts his gaze around the room, then continues, "I am Richard Henry Walker, Henry to many, and along with Doctor Liang and Investigator Arnold, we represent Canfield."

Antonio slowly stands, then as he raises his glass states, "I am Commander Antonio Rossi. With me is Marco, my trusted officer."

Ken stands, mumbles, "I am Ken of Aqua." He sits down immediately.

Dianne stands, then fills the room with her confident voice, "I am Dianne, I am here representing the council of elders."

Ken is stunned by her statement, then as he stares at her, it dawns on him just how historic this meeting is.

Henry takes a deep breath then states, "Let me begin this by being brief. Between us all, we represent around a quarter of a million people, people who trust us and rely on us for their safety."

Those around the room nod their heads as Henry continues, "In summary, Canfield, along with the other protected cities, has technology, Golem One has heavy manufacturing facilities, while Aqua has the only water treatment facility with the capacity to service everyone. Now, if Antonio's fleet would join us, we could seek out a new place to live."

Antonio stands, then glances to Marco as he nods, before stating, "We'll join you!" He feels an excitement like never before.

Joe suddenly remembers what Marco had told him, then exclaims, "What about the pirates?"

The room turns at Joe's outburst, then looks back to Antonio as he replies, "Once our ships are repaired, and equipped with weapons, they'll be no match for us."

Dianne's eyes narrow as she questions, "You want us to provide you with weapons?"

Antonio sighs as he responds, "I know how this looks, and I know we've raided communities too, but," he pauses and looks around the room before he continues, "if they come, we're the only thing standing in their way. So, unless you think you can sink their ships with your remaining bombs..." He leaves the statement hanging.

Dianne bites at her bottom lip, pondering, then motions to Jerry as she says, "Trust has to start somewhere. I will discuss arming the fleet with the other communities."

Henry glances to Dianne, then rubs his hands together eagerly as he says, "We could allocate auto-cops to each ship as well."

Antonio feels a chill run up his spine; the idea of robots on his ships bothers him, then upon seeing Marco and Jerry conversing together, he relaxes. He trusts Marco's judgment, so he nods as he responds, "You can put your robots on the ships the pirates are likely to try to take, like the flagship and tanker."

Dianne nods to Antonio as she goes to her list of questions, "During your travels, did you find anywhere that looked habitable?"

"Many years ago, like over a hundred and fifty, our fleet found a massive base on an island. It was untouched, before we stripped it bare. According to rumors, the crew worked out in the open, safe!

158

When I was a lad, I saw a few places where there was no gas, but they were no more than rocky atolls rising from the ocean. Pretty much every other landmass we've found, looks like yours, covered in deadly gas, or worse."

"Worse?" She questions, wondering what could be worse.

"Yeah," Antonio replies, "and you don't want to know. Trust me on that."

"We should go back to that base you found and see what the surrounding area is like." Dianne suggests.

Antonio lowers his gaze as he half mumbles, admitting, "Um. We don't really know where it is."

"Well," Dianne replies with a smile, "we have extensive pre-war maps! I'm sure we could figure it out."

Antonio lifts his gaze as he asks, "I'm not sure what you hope to find. If the stories the lads tell are only half-true, there's nothing left."

Dianne waves her hand to indicate everyone in the room as she replies, "It would be a great way to start our joint operations. Don't you think?"

Antonio replies slowly, reluctantly admitting, "We don't have the fuel for any decent trek."

Joe surprises everyone when he stands and says, "It's true, the fleet is just about dead in the water. But," he pauses as he smiles at Henry, "I'm sure that Canfield could repair the fuel-cell units."

Henry puts his hands together in front of his face as he considers Joe's comment. After a moment, he lowers his hands and says, "I am unfamiliar with the technology, but if we have the capability, it will be done." He stares at Antonio, measuring the man as he ponders what he will do with a repaired fleet, one with weapons and fuel.

159

Antonio grins excitedly as he slaps Marco on the back, saying, "Can you imagine it? Last month we were drifting aimlessly at sea, and now we're going to go on a real mission, not just some raid, but a mission with a purpose."

Ken frowns as he asks, "How's your fresh water supplied?"

Antonio is still grinning as he replies, "The flagship's fuel-cells which convert seawater into fuel, also desalinizes it, which lets us supply the fleet with fresh water."

"We should install a freshwater system on every ship." Ken offers, surprising everyone.

Dianne frown as she asks, "Is that really necessary?"

"Yes!" Ken states bluntly.

Henry glances around the room, then nods as he says, "I agree."

The talks continue for hours, during which time they all come to realize just how fragile their lives are. Every dome and underground facility has some sort of age related issue, with some near failure point. Canfield is not the only city which utilizes augmented reality to keep their citizens from knowing the truth either, further complicating things.

Henry has been listening and absorbing everything he hears. After much thinking, he stands, then states, "We should consolidate the people, and abandon the smaller communities, thus conserving our efforts. Canfield has the capacity to take in almost fifty thousand, which would more than double our population. What about the others?" He asks, directing his question to Dianne.

"Golem One could take in almost ten thousand more, but, if the three outlying communities are brought in, that would push the rest to capacity." She replies.

Henry puts his hands behind his back as he paces the room, sharing his thoughts, "Canfield's outer dome could be repaired, now that we have less to fear of a pirate attack. It's also the closest dome to Golem One, making the city a logical staging point, should we find habitable land."

Antonio smiles as he shares his thoughts, "Who would have thought that we would be sitting here, discussing an alliance, after all that has happened?"

"Not an alliance, Antonio." Henry responds as he looks around, adding "This is more than a simple alliance, this is all of us becoming one."

Antonio frowns as he questions, "One what?"

"One people."

"One?" Antonio repeats, still unclear what he means.

Henry walks around the room as he expands on his thoughts, "Right now we represent the outlying communities, Canfield, Aqua, pirates…"

"Steady on with the pirate thing." Antonio interrupts lightheartedly.

"Sea-faring people!" Henry offers as he lifts his eyebrows, then continues, "My point is; we need to create a single title for us all!"

Dianne considers the pre-war maps she has, then offers her thoughts, "We need to avoid the old-world adages if we are to have a fresh start."

Antonio grins as he suggests, "Let's just see what we find! Perhaps a name will come to mind then?"

Dianne frowns as something she heard earlier comes to mind, "What about these other communities you used to raid? We should visit them."

Antonio sighs, then looking at Marco says, "I don't know where they are; the old command crew is dead, and they took much of their knowledge with them."

Marco nods as he adds his thoughts, "All I know is that they exist, but as for where, that's a mystery. Besides, all they could ever offer was clothing, food, and water."

The talks continue for some time as they discuss not only the complete refit of the fleet, but of the food and water situation, along with the technologies available to them.

It is late in the evening when something suddenly occurs to Joe. He blurts out, "Oh my! I never considered why the supermarkets only had a few types of cereal, or that cans of vegetables only came in a couple of brands."

Henry nods as he responds, "Golem One was responsible for making sure each community had enough, all we did was send Canfield's surplus to them."

Joe's jaw drops as it dawns on him that Canfield does not even have its own warehouses! He frowns as he asks, "What about things like shoes, watches, computers?"

Dianne stands as she answers, "Each community has some technical manufacturing; as for cans and boxes, the packaging centers simply change the labels." She paces as she explains, "Our archives tell us that immediately following the great war, key facilities were either covered or moved underground. Small domes were hastily built over farms and industrial complexes, with the larger domes being built over these. The gas, as we have all seen, hovers close to the ground, thus they had a little time to enclose them fully."

Antonio puts his hand to his chin as he deliberates sharing what he knows. He reluctantly speaks, "During our travels, according to the lads anyway, we came across literally hundreds of failed dome cities." He gulps, then says, "Some were destroyed during raids by pirate fleets, others, just failed." He looks around panicky as he quickly adds, "None of us alive have raided a city!"

Henry grins as he leans back in his chair, and says, "And yet you were going to raid Canfield!"

Antonio shakes his head as he explains, "Actually, we were coming to see if you would help! Our previous Commander would have taken what he needed, regardless of the consequences to you all. I had to kill him, in the hopes that we could end the vicious cycle of raiding just to stay alive for a little longer." He looks around, letting his words sink in.

Dianne smiles warmly as she says, "And here we are, discussing a union of forces, for the good of all of us!"

The talks continue for some time, until finally everyone is satisfied that progress is being made. The meeting finally ends, allowing them to retire to their rooms.

Later in the evening, when all is quiet, Henry goes to Dianne's room.

Dianne feels drained by the day's events and with a sigh, asks, "Whatever you want, can't it wait?"

Henry smiles as he replies, "We could repair the fleet's heavy guns, if..." He pauses as he looks up and down the corridor, then for effect, adds, "...if, we put auto-cops on those ships too."

She motions for him to enter her room as she questions, "What would that do? How can they can stop the ships from firing at us?" Dianne presses, adding, "My understanding of the ship's guns is that they fire heavy projectiles, and once fired nothing can stop them."

Henry steps inside, then shuts the door. Grinning wolfishly, he lowers his voice as he says, "Yes, but I think the firing mechanism is electronic, which if it is, means we can do something to protect ourselves."

"I see." She replies slowly, then as a scowl develops, presses, "How can we be sure of our safety?"

"We could add an undetectable circuit, which we pre-program to prevent the guns from targeting whatever we want. The auto-cops would simply be a failsafe measure."

Dianne's jaw drops, "That might work."

Henry takes a deep breath, then says, "One more thing. I noticed that Jerry's well-polished gun, is old."

Dianne flinches, then reluctantly admits, "Small arms were manufactured in another facility, and when it fell, we lost the ability to make more."

"Why didn't you tell me this before?"

"I didn't want anyone to know that Golem One is almost defenseless."

"What about the heavy guns on the way in?" Henry asks, tales of them fresh on his mind.

Dianne lowers her gaze as she replies, "They have a few shots each, but we can't make more. We put all of our efforts into maintaining the nuclear deterrent."

"Well," Henry replies, "Canfield can build an assembly plant for more weapons. Golem One must stand!"

The pair discusses details long into the night, neither realizing that Maggie is wide awake in the next room, listening intently to everything.

Canfield Switches Off

Doctor Liang, Arnold, and Henry sit nervously in their chairs. The time has come to tell the people of Canfield the truth.

Doctor Liang shakes his head as he comments, "Every study we have, shows that the people will riot!"

Arnold sighs as he says what they already know, "We don't have enough auto-cops to handle a city-wide civil disturbance."

Henry nods as he replies, "None of the communities do, but we know this has to be done. So, let's do it!"

All across the city and in the smaller domes attached to Canfield, every monitor, television screen, and electronic public billboard, switches to an image indicating that a public announcement is coming. Liang had convinced them to choose Sunday, as most of the citizens would be in their own homes, thus minimizing the risk of people gathering and causing trouble.

Across the continent, the other communities with which Golem One works, are also told of the newly formed alliance. Although some already know more than others about the world, it was decided to share the same information with every community.

Henry stares at his scripted speech, then begins, "I am senior medical director Richard Henry Walker, and I have an important message for all of you. Four hundred years ago, the world was embroiled in a great war. History records us as the victors, but in truth, no one won. We all lost!" He stops and stares at the cameras as his mind races, imagining the citizen's reactions as they listen.

Arnold discreetly prods Henry to continue.

Henry clears his throat, then continues, "Since then, we have been living on borrowed time. Our country does not have millions of citizens, but mere thousands, most of whom live here, in Canfield, under a protective dome. The land outside the dome is inhospitable, and unable to support life. We're going to shut down the augmented implants which each citizen has, for a moment, so that you may see for yourselves."

Doctor Liang taps on his console, deactivating the augment software. He waits ten seconds, then reenables the complex program.

Henry swallows hard, then continues, "There is hope. A fleet of ships is to begin a mission of exploration. They're going to search for a new place, a safe place, where we may prosper. In the interim, life will continue as it has, with the exception that we are now committing our efforts to the fleet's success."

Doctor Liang switches the cameras off, then shrugs as he says, "Now to see how the populace takes that."

They do not have to wait long before reports of civil disturbances begin to pour in.

Arnold shakes his head as he quickly skims each report, then breathes a sigh of relief. He whispers, "Quite a lot of minor accidents from people who became confused, along with a few reports of vandalism." He keeps skimming then stops cold, adding, "Sadly, we have reports of suicides now."

The men go quiet as the reports of civil unrest increase.

The auto-cops are kept busy for days, managing numerous incidents, and for the first time in living memory, have a backlog of issues to deal with. The auto-fixers are busier still, repairing damage from vandalism and accidents, alike.

The three men spend their time monitoring any incident which seems likely to escalate, and then personally respond. The absentee rate skyrockets as many people quit going to work. Fortunately, the suicides are limited to a handful of people.

By the end of the week, life returns to a semblance of normalcy, as people realize that damaging the very city which supports them, is ludicrous. Some people go without power for days, while others lose their dwellings due to the poor judgment of a few.

Henry keeps in contact with Dianne and is pleased to learn that all the communities are coming to terms with the truth.

The Island

Finding the island with the abandoned base was easier than expected. Dianne's pre-war maps had listed a few possible locations, reducing their search time. The hard part had been repairing the fleet, especially the overhaul and replacement of their ancient engines. To perform these tasks, a massive dock was hastily built, then covered. An airlock system was installed allowing people to work in relative safety, while others came and went as they needed. In addition, Henry committed almost every auto-fixer Canfield could spare to the effort, eventually providing over one hundred units.

New pipes and plumbing were installed throughout the fleet, including fresh toilets and showers. Water filtration systems were added to each ship, taking the load off the carrier, and eliminating the need to transfer water between ships. However, it was the installation of new bilge pumps which proved to be the greatest morale boost for the ship's crews.

Thanks to the auto-fixers from Canfield, the steel from Golem One, and components from just about every community, the repairs only took four months! During this time, the ship's heavy weapons were also replaced, something the crew had been betting would not get done. Much to their surprise, newly manufactured sixteen-inch shells were delivered, along with replacement gun barrels and lift systems.

Personal weapons are in short supply, so only a few people have been lucky enough to get one. As for the plane, it still rests on the frozen elevator,

169

as removing it served no purpose, besides, it has become something of a symbol to the crew.

It had taken Dianne weeks to convince the council of elders to agree to all the refits, especially the heavy weapons, with the discussions becoming quite heated at times. They eventually agreed that without the fleet, they were effectively trapped. Although they could build their own ships, doing so would be a difficult task, requiring more resources than they could spare.

Much to Antonio's surprise, one of the smaller outlying communities, Perkville, still utilizes diesel generators in preference to solar energy, and even has a small-scale refinery near an oil field. Luckily for the fleet, the people of Perkville are fully aware of the world they live in, and not only do they manufacture heavy-duty diesel engines, they also supply fuel to all the communities attached to Golem One.

Henry is one of a handful of people who knew that Canfield, a solar powered city, had backup generators, but even he did not know where the fuel came from. He had thought Golem One provided everything and is as surprised as the others to learn of Perkville's contributions.

It did not take long to replace the ship's patched-up fuel tanks, and to fill them to the brim. The tanker's massive hold took the longest time to prepare, but it now sits low in the water, its holding tanks full of fuel. The carrier's fuel cell units are also now fully operational, their fuel output far less than the fleet's consumption rate, but still a respectable amount, especially when compared to before the repairs. The solar panels which line the carrier's deck have been replaced with the same units which cover the tops of the domes, another element the bulk of the citizens are oblivious to.

At first, the crews were suspicious of the machines which rove their ships. But, they soon came to realize that the auto-cops and auto-fixers work in tandem, isolating areas which need repair, thus protecting the crew from any potential harm.

The fleet sounds different now, the engines smoother and quieter. A steady thrum runs through the carrier, a far cry from the raggedy chugging the crew was used to. The engines are far more efficient too, an unexpected bonus. They left the coast off Golem One a month ago, traversing the ocean waves with ease. For the last hundred years or so, the fleet followed the ocean currents, whereas now, the ships confidently slice through the waves, heading into territories unexplored for generations.

Antonio points through the fresh glass on the bridge of the flagship at the naval base ahead of them. There is no mist hovering over the land, or the water in the area; in fact, trees, shrubs, and grass has overgrown much of the base, while birds fly overhead. They all stare at the birds in bewilderment; none of them has ever seen a bird, except for Joe and Henry who saw the virtual ones in Canfield. Small waves crash onto the shore, free of any rubbish or debris.

Paul and Freddie issue orders to the crew, and the other ships, as they maneuver through the narrowing straights. Though no orders were given by Antonio, the fleet slows as they get closer to the landmass.

Henry, Joe, and Marco, stand alongside Antonio, all of them gazing at the dilapidated base. Its storage tanks have long since collapsed in on themselves, as have all the buildings, except for one single story dwelling with a flat roof.

Marco squints, trying to discern details, then says, "Well, it's not quite how I was expecting it to look."

Henry motions to the island as he suggests, "It's pretty big, we should still check it out."

Antonio has been considering the reefs in the area, well-aware of his officer's diligence, then nods in agreement as he orders, "Halt the fleet; we're going ashore."

Massive cranes which once stood tall, have long since collapsed, their rusting vestiges adding to the bleak landscape. Rust streaks down the side of the docks where water has flowed, eroding deep grooves into the once thick metal. The collapsed buildings form mounds, dotting the landscape like anthills. A bent flagpole sways in the breeze, the flag itself long since gone.

The three transports from the flagship push seaweed aside as they make their way to shore, disturbing schools of fish in the process. They arrive at the beach and position themselves with weapons covering each side, flanking and protecting the central transport.

After a few tense moments, Joe, Henry, Antonio, Marco, and Jerry, step ashore from the central transport. Marco holds his new weapon proudly; a copy of Jerry's. Thanks to his months of training, he has become quite proficient in its use.

The two well-armed men walk on either side of the others, their weapons sweeping the thick foliage as they make their way toward the remaining building. Leaves and dirt cover the ground, while grass pokes through the deep cracks in the concrete. Shrubs have encroached from the base edges, nature having reclaimed the outlying buildings. Stains of oil mark the ground like dark fingers where it leaked from the ruined storage tanks.

Henry takes out his Geiger counter, a gift from Golem One, then after checking the readings, relaxes. He gives the group a nod, indicating that the radiation levels are safe.

Marco shakes his head as he says, "There's nothing here for us."

Jerry replies, his eyes still scanning the forest's edge, "I wouldn't be so sure. A base this large may have an underground complex."

"Underwater you mean!" Marco replies bluntly, motioning to the waves.

"This is old architecture, pre-war!" Jerry replies, adding, "You never know."

While the others discuss the base, Joe stops and stares at a nearby tree. A squirrel runs haphazardly up and down the tree trunk, its tail twitching as it stares at the interlopers, clearly agitated by their presence. He smiles as he watches the little animal collect a few nuts, then retreat high into the tree's branches.

"You coming?" Jerry's question intrudes on Joe's thoughts, bringing him back to the task at hand.

Joe grins as he replies, "Real animals, no poison gas, and clean beaches." He grins as he adds, "I was worried the entire world was like where we're from."

The group makes their way to the remaining building, its flat roof is covered with dirt and debris with grass growing on it. Jerry leads the way through the open doors, his weapon ready. He stops as his eyes adjust to the dim light which filters in through the filthy and shattered windows alike. The fact that any are intact, surprises him more than the thick layer of dust and dirt which covers the floor. He turns his flashlight on and shines it around the room. The main area has half a dozen small rooms lining two of the walls, each with a ruined table and chair. The remnants of computer consoles litter the floor, where they fell when their tables crumbled.

The rest of the group follows, their own lights shining hazily through the dust their feet kick up.

Joe motions to the side rooms as he says, "This looks like it was an admin building, with those small rooms being offices."

Jerry taps the wall as he says, "Pretty heavy duty for an office building though!"

Joe shrugs as he offers, "Perhaps the weather is bad here."

Antonio chimes in, "Oh, we've been in some pretty hellacious storms!"

Henry frowns as he examines the rooms, then as he puts his hands on his hips, he says, "If this was the main building, then there should be files somewhere."

"Probably stored in those." Joe ventures as he motions to the useless computers.

"Hey!" Marco shouts, getting their attention, "Check it out!"

They rush over to where Marco is cleaning a thick layer of dust off a glass display, inside which is a huge map of the base. They stare at the map, excited, then frown.

"What language is that?" Marco asks; the symbols and words though legible, are alien to him.

Jerry shakes his head as he replies, "I have no idea."

Marco points proudly to an area on the map as he says, "You're right! I don't need to know the language to know what that means. This place does have underground storage tanks."

Antonio snorts, "But after all this time, I'm pretty sure they're useless."

"Not if they're stainless." Marco replies, lifting his eyebrows.

Antonio frowns as he asks, "I doubt if they have anything in them. The Fleet Commander who found this place took everything, or so we were told."

Jerry looks around as a disturbing thought comes to mind. Hesitantly, he asks, "Antonio, the story goes that your fleet found this place around a hundred and seventy years ago."

"That's right." Antonio replies as he turns to look at Jerry.

"And this place had been here, abandoned, for over two hundred years when your people found it." He presses.

"Crazy, isn't it!" Antonio replies with a grin.

'No," Jerry responds bluntly as his frown deepens, "It's impossible!"

"Why do you say that?" Antonio replies, his grin fading.

Jerry waves his hands around as he states, "Because storage tanks don't last that long. Fifty years maybe, but not two hundred."

"What are you saying?" Antonio presses, his curiosity aroused.

"The entire story of finding this place, abandoned. It just doesn't make sense." Jerry states bluntly, adding, "Look at the overgrowth, the rust, it's not four hundred years' worth. I think this was a thriving community when your Commander found it. I am also willing to bet they were trading fuel for food after the war. It looks like they had plenty!"

Antonio turns to Marco as he asks, "Have you heard anything like this?"

Marco shakes his head, then slowly admits, "The story of finding this place, abandoned, and yet in great shape, does sound far-fetched now."

Jerry looks around as he shares his thoughts out loud, "I doubt we'll ever know the truth." With a sigh he adds, "But I'm certain the underground tanks are useless."

"Let's find out." Marco presses as he taps the glass covered map.

It does not take them long to find the storage tanks, the map shows them all quite clearly. They are buried deep beneath the ground and accessed by concrete stairways which terminate at solid doors. Each door is forced open, to reveal the same scene time and time again.

Antonio checks the last one, then says, "Yep, just like the others. It's caved in on itself, and dry as a bone!"

Jerry shines his light along the edge of the pit, adding, "These concrete enclosures were designed to preventing any spill from reaching the ocean."

Marco rubs his chin as he ventures, "Well, that would match your theory Jerry."

Henry stands nearby with his hands on his hips looking around, perplexed. He says, "We're missing something."

Antonio shrugs as he replies, "Look, I don't know what happened here. I only know what we were told."

Henry shakes his head as he shares his thoughts, "No, no, it's not about your people, it's about this base. It's too big to simply be a storage depot for ships."

Jerry shrugs as he suggests, "I'm pretty sure we're alone. We would cover more ground if we spilt up and search the island."

"Sounds good." Henry replies, gaining a nod from Antonio.

The search reveals a pair of small oil derricks, along with the remnants of a refinery, hidden between some low hills. Elsewhere on the island a complex series of pipework is found, running through the undergrowth from the refinery to the underground tanks they searched earlier.

Meeting back up, they share what they found during their exploration, each of them describing in detail what they saw, and then offering their own theories as to the base's purpose.

Henry listens to everyone, then glancing at the setting sun, says, "I want to look at that map one more time, before we go back to the ships."

"What do you hope to find?" Marco queries, looking around the at the crumbling structures.

"I'm not sure, yet."

They hurry to the building, where Henry cleans more of the dust and dirt off the glass case, then scrutinizes the edges of map. He smiles when he notices little dotted lines radiating from the island to the edge of the map. He puts his hands together as Marco holds a flash light on the map.

Marco's impatience gets the best of him as he asks, "Whatcha thinking?"

Henry turns to Joe and asks, "Do these look like trade routes to you?"

"Oh my. Yes!"

"Well then, if my theory is correct, this is a supply depot."

"Some supply depot!" Joe exclaims.

Henry taps the edge of the map and says, "We should go there!"

They all lean in closer, and then notice what Henry saw; dozens of dotted lines converge on an area just before the map ends, with only one of those going from the island they are on.

Marco frowns, then says, "I don't get it. Why there?"

Henry taps the glass as he explains, "This map shows this island in great detail, and goes to a lot of trouble to show numerous supply lines, while this base only had one. A base this large should have had many, unless it was built for one purpose."

"What do you think this place was used for?" Marco presses.

"A refueling center for something big, judging by the size of the cranes." Henry replies as he looks around.

They return to the flagship, then spend the night checking copies of old maps that Dianne had provided for them. It takes them a little while to figure out where the routes are going, but when they do they are all stunned.

Jerry nods as he says, "I knew there was a moon base! And we just found a launch facility for it."

Henry adds his thoughts, "We should check it out!"

"Ya think?" Antonio blurts with a hint of sarcasm, adding, "We'll head out with sunrise and high tide."

Joe asks excitedly, "Does anyone know what we expect to find?"

They all shake their heads, or mumble that they have no idea. Some of them sleep well, but for others, sleep is elusive as they wonder what they will discover. High tide follows the morning sun, allowing them to leave the way they came without fear of running aground.

Though they know where to go, their destination is quite a distance away, with many islands and atolls in between.

Chapter Nine – New Frontiers

They have traveled more these last few months than in Antonio's entire lifetime. They explore islands and atolls, while steadily moving farther and farther away from Golem One, as they head in the direction the lines on the map indicated.

The fleet sails into a deep harbor unmolested, the third one since leaving the base where they found the map. Each time they stopped, they found the same thing; a base long since abandoned, with either massive airstrips or impressive dockyards. But in each instance, there was nothing of value left.

A thin layer of mist hovers over the water, but not the landmass ahead. Huge domes dot the landscape, along with a large radio antenna, its array pointing upward. An enormous rust-encrusted rail line runs along the ground, then sweeps its way up a mountainside, nearly going vertical.

Henry proudly states, "The old launch facility to the moon!"

"Halt the fleet!" Antonio orders, "Send the landing party. Standard configuration."

Paul and Freddie relay the orders, having become quite adept at the procedure, improving it with each exploration. The ship's crew has everything ready in minutes, all they are waiting on is the landing party.

Jerry and Marco make sure the landing site is safe, before relaxing and allowing the others to get out. This facility is not on an easily checked island, but instead is on the coast of a massive continent, thus adding to their caution. The two men expand their search, checking each building carefully, before moving on.

Marco casts his gaze across the landscape, then says, "I can't believe this place wasn't levelled during the war!"

Henry waves his Geiger counter around, then frowns as he rechecks the readings. He sighs as he says, "It looks like this place was hit with a neutron bomb, but it's okay, the residual radiation is negligible now."

Joe tilts his head as he asks, "Neutron bomb?"

"Dianne told me about them when she handed me this unit," Henry replies as he holds the Geiger counter up. He looks at the landscape as he explains, "They're bombs which do little damage to structures, but their intense radiation kills all life!"

The remains of those who were at the facility when the bomb hit, dot the landscape. Their bones poke through the decayed remnants of clothing, trapping dust, and over time forming small mounds, providing each victim their own personal burial plot. There are hundreds of mounds scattered about the facility, subduing their excitement over finding the place.

Jerry interrupts their thoughts when he shouts out, "I think I've found the control room."

The building is a large two story, with its upper level full of broken windows. The lower level has no windows at all, requiring them to turn their flashlights on to look around.

Joe grins as he stands before the vast array of decaying computer monitors. Looking around he says, "It's a pity we have no way of knowing what happened to the moon base."

Henry wanders around the ancient control room, then sighs as he agrees, "If the historical documents are at all close to the truth, they had a vast facility."

Joe's light drifts over the wall ahead. He freezes as his eyes lock on a series of deep grooves. "Wow!" he exclaims loudly.

Henry spins around, alarmed, then relaxes when he sees the message on the wall, "It's a radio frequency!" He states excitedly.

Joe looks upward as he asks, "It couldn't be for them? Could it?"

"There is only one way to find out." Henry replies as he jots the numbers down.

Antonio walks to the wall and runs his fingers along the grooves, examining them carefully. He casts his appraising gaze around the dilapidated room, then nods as he says, "If you wanted to leave a lasting message, then this is how it's done!"

Henry motions to Gordon as he says, "Do you think we could build a transmitter?"

Jerry grins as he adds his thoughts, "No need. Golem One has one, it's how we keep in contact with all the communities."

Henry's jaw drops, "I thought we used a land-line."

"We have both." Jerry replies with a shrug.

Joe's eyebrows lift as he states, "I thought you knew everything!"

"Apparently not!" Henry responds, adding, "We need to send a message, to see if anyone is still up there."

"No way anyone is still alive." Marco states, adding his thoughts.

Joe tilts his head as he questions, "Why not? I never thought I lived in a dome! Few of us thought Aqua existed, or the fleet, so why not a moon base?"

Marco shakes his head as he puts his hands on his hips, stating, "For starters, Aqua was using the ocean to make fresh water, and as for the rest of us, we still relied on the planet for air. The moon has none of that."

Henry lifts a finger, smiles, then says, "Well, we should still send a message, to find out."

Marco looks around the room, then says, "Even if there are survivors, they won't want to talk to us."

Antonio puts his hand on the deep marks in the wall as he responds, "They did once, or they wouldn't have left this."

Joe looks around once more, then says, "What about the huge antenna that's outside?"

Jerry recalls the antenna as he ponders the possibility, then shakes his head, replying, "We would have to power it up, then hope it works and that's is pointed the right way. No, it's easier to go to Golem One and try from there."

Antonio considers where they are, in relation to Golem One, then says, "We're close to three weeks out, unless we run at full speed, then it's a little over a week. But that would burn a lot more fuel!"

Henry glances around, then says, "I don't see how a couple of extra weeks will be an issue; the moon base is either good, or not."

Exploring the rest of the facility offers few surprises. A pair of massive carts, which are clearly designed to run along the rail, rest inside a dilapidated building. Farther out, a field of underground storage tanks is discovered, but as with every storage tank found to date, they are ruined.

They explore the area for two days before deciding it is time to head back to Golem One.

There is much debate amongst the crews as to whether the moon base still has people who have survived.

Battle Royale

Antonio sprints to the bridge, his mid-day lunch having been interrupted by a ship wide alarm. Breathing heavily, he gasps, "What's going on?"

Marco simply points ahead, his expression stern. Paul and Freddie had alerted the rest of the fleet the moment they saw smoke on the horizon, and ordered all ships to slow, and to begin to turn away.

A rag-tag assortment of forty ships is on an intercept course, their objective is quite clear, they are rushing toward them at high speed.

"Attack!" Antonio shouts loudly, shot-gunning his orders, "Turn the fleet north. Full-speed! Get some distance between us."

Joe stares at the approaching fleet, then asks, "How do you know they're hostile?"

Antonio points at them as he says, "All that smoke coming out of their stacks means they're running hard, and no one runs old ships like that, unless they mean business."

Antonio's fleet is not a coordinated force. The old cruise liner turns slowly, while the battleship before it turns much harder, and faster, cutting in front of the liner's path.

The captain of the cruise liner stares wide-eyed as the battleship crosses their path. He bellows, "Emergency stop! Emergency stop!"

Meanwhile, the captain of the battleship is staring the other way at the approaching fleet, oblivious to the liner bearing down on him as he orders, "Fire all weapons!"

Moments later the deck shakes as three one-ton shells loudly thunder from their barrels,

Seconds later, the ship is shaken once more as three more, equally loud shells, exit the rear turrets. The crew is stunned by the noise; it is far louder than the single test shots which were fired when the barrels were replaced. They watch and wait as the shells sail across the sky, all the while the cruise liner is still aimed straight at them.

"Captain!" Screams an officer on the battleship as he points to the dangerously close liner.

"Flank speed!" Orders the captain, his eyes wide as he sees the vessel bearing down on his ship. "Turn her about, get her ass out of their way!"

The battleship speeds up, and begins to turn, swinging her rear away from the approaching liner, which is slowing, and also turning away, putting the ship directly across the path of the entire fleet, and pointing them back toward the approaching force.

The second battleship fires its weapons from behind the liner, the shells narrowly missing the liner's upper decks, further rattling the crew. Antonio stares at the chaos, a chill running up his spine as he watches his fleet turning and speeding up at differing rates. He can only watch as the liner narrowly misses the rear of the battleship, and flounders in its wake as it slows. The flagship is also still turning and narrowly misses the rear of the liner.

The liner's captain stares at the approaching armada fearfully, then bellows, "Swing us about, then go to flank speed!"

The first volley of shells passes harmlessly over the approaching fleet, creating huge splashes in the water with each impact. The gun crews adjust their aim, then fire again. They are not well-practiced in the use of the ship's main guns, thus the two battleships fire shots at sporadic intervals.

Shells splash the water, with some impacting near the approaching force. One of the ships is showered with water as one impacts close to them.

"The guns can't go any lower!" Marco shouts as he watches the battleships fire another volley.

Antonio looks back at the cruise liner, then grins as he replies, "But we're faster than them."

Marco glances back and smiles widely; the liner is pushing her engines to the maximum. Thick black smoke pours from her stacks, but she is slowly catching up.

The approaching fleet slows, then turns away, but not before a single shell finds its mark. One of the smaller ships is hit directly above the water line. The impact is staggering. Shell fragments exit the far side of the vessel, taking with it everything in its path. The vessel has no chance; its back breaks. The two halves, though still connected by the upper workings, twist and turn independently as the vessel sinks into the ocean depths, taking her crew with her.

"Cease fire!" Antonio orders.

Marco relays the order, then laments, "But, we could sink them all!"

Antonio glances to Joe and Henry, then says, "We fired, what, thirty, forty rounds? And hit one ship!"

Marco responds slowly, "Ah, yes."

"That's about a third of our compliment of shells!" Antonio states bluntly.

BOOM!

The explosion from one of the retreating ships, though muffled, is still loud. The ship begins to list to one side as flames flicker from its collapsing smoke stacks.

Joe's jaw drops as he stares at the ship, and the crew members who decide to jump into the water instead of burning alive.

Freddie cringes as he shares what they are all thinking, "Burned, gassed, or drowned." He swallows hard as he adds, "None are good ways to go."

No one responds as they watch, too far away to help even if they wanted to. The ship and crew are abandoned to their fate. The floundering ship begins to take on water from some unseen damage, and then sinks. It slides beneath the waves, leaving a pool of debris in its wake. Survivors splash in the water for a while, but soon succumb to the effects of the gas.

Joe frowns as a thought comes to mind. He glances around, then says, "If we're going home, and those other ships are in the way, how do we get around them?"

Antonio grins as he replies, "It's an old trick, but it's a good one. Just watch." He motions to the bridge crew, then smiles with pride as they get to work. This is a maneuver the fleet has practiced.

A man climbs to the top of the flagship's tower, where he watches the retreating force through powerful binoculars. After a short while he begins yelling and shouting.

Antonio grins as he orders, "Smoke 'em up boys."

Joe watches as each ship discharges more smoke, a lot more smoke, and then begin a slow turn back the way they came. The fleet is travelling at the same speed as the flagship, which although is at full speed, is slower than their actual maximums.

Around twenty minutes later the man in the lookout begins shouting and waving once more. Antonio nods to Freddie and Paul, then smiles as they relay his silent orders.

The fleet begins to slow, as does the amount of smoke pouring into the sky. After a few more minutes the fleet turns back to their original heading, while the amount of smoke which leaves each vessel is negligible.

Antonio grins, "Their lookouts will think we're headed back from where we came; they won't find us again."

It is late in the afternoon by the time they reach the area where the two ships sank; flotsam, oil, and a handful of bodies are all that remain.

Freddie frowns as something in the distance catches his eye. He grabs a pair of binoculars, then searches at the horizon, looking for what caught his eye.

"Ship! Dead in the water." Freddie states, his eyes locked on the target.

Antonio narrows his eyes as he considers what to do. He then orders, "Approach slowly; keep a good watch out. It could be a ruse."

Freddie and Paul relay orders to the fleet, and in short order have the flagship leading the way, flanked by both battleships, with the rest of the fleet trailing a little behind. The closer they get to the floundering vessel, the less it appears to be a trap.

Joe stares at the ship in dismay. A gaping hole is ripped into its side, with jagged metal pealing outward. Obviously, something inside blew out. The ship is caked in black smudges, signs the crew extinguished a fierce fire. A handful of people stand on the deck of the ruined ship, waving frantically.

"Leave 'em!" Antonio orders; his tone flat and emotionless.

Joe's jaw drops in dismay as he states, "You can't leave them like that!"

"Why not?" Antonio counters, "They would have boarded this ship and killed us all without a second thought."

"They're still people," Joe replies, "and if we're to start a new society, we need to learn how to bring in groups like them."

Antonio turns to Freddie and Paul, then upon seeing them shrug, he looks to Marco for support.

Marco's face twitches involuntarily as he debates with himself between what has always been done, and Joe's statement. After a moment he reluctantly admits, "Joe has a point, but I follow your orders, Commander!"

Antonio scowls, "Marco, bring 'em aboard" Then he grins as an idea comes to mind, "Get those auto-cops to watch 'em!"

"Aye, aye, Sir!"

It takes a while to rescue the helpless survivors, but they do. They are led to a rarely used section of the ship, where a combination of armed guards and Canfield's auto-cops watch them. None of those rescued offer any resistance, and although they are happy to be rescued, they are apprehensive about what will happen to them.

Marco returns to the bridge and reports, "Thirty-seven survivors; twenty-eight men and nine women."

Antonio nods as he replies, "Good, now let's get going." He has not been happy that the fleet has been stationary for so long, especially with the hostile force out there.

Paul and Freddie begin relaying orders to the fleet, and soon have them underway. Joe smiles at the report of the people rescued, then begins to feel self-conscious; Antonio is staring at him, and has been for a while.

"The newcomers will be Joe's responsibility!" Antonio states, adding as he motions, "It was after all, your idea to bring them aboard."

Joe blinks a few times, surprised, then says, "I'll go and check on them right now!"

It takes Joe quite a bit longer than it took Marco to traverse the same distance; he takes a few wrong turns along the way, but eventually finds himself face to face with the survivors. Joe's jaw drops as he looks at the group. Their clothes are torn and tattered, barely covering their emaciated bodies. None of the captives look his way, but instead shuffle away, fearfully.

"Get these people some food and water!" Joe demands, anger building in his voice for the first time in years.

"Not until I'm ordered to!" Replies a surly guard.

"I'm ordering you!" Joe shouts.

The guard picks at his rotten and broken teeth, ignoring Joe's comment. He spits on the floor as his colleagues snicker.

"Half rations for you. Idiot!" Marco's loud voice cuts through the air like a knife, causing them all to jump.

"I don't take orders from the likes of him!" The guard scowls, motioning to Joe with his thumb.

The other guards move aside as Marco steps to the man and then, without warning, snatches his weapon. The man stares at his empty hands, as if in shock, then looks up and stares at Marco with hate filled eyes. He tilts his head left and right, cracking his neck as his rage builds.

Perhaps it was Marco's smile, or his slight shrug, which put the man over the edge, either way, the fight starts and ends with one swing, and one punch.

"Put that idiot with the prisoners!" Marco orders as he shakes his fist. The man's jaw was harder than he had expected.

The other guards comply immediately, with two of them scurrying off.

Marco nods to the remaining guards as he states, "Fleet Commander Antonio specifically ordered this man, Joe, to see to the needs of the people we rescued. Defying his orders is treason!"

"We didn't know!" Stammers one of the guards.

Marco sneers, "And now you do!"

Joe does not like it that he is the cause of all the trouble, and says, "Marco, It's just a misunderstanding. They really had no way of knowing."

Marco grins as he replies, "Oh, they knew!"

The stammering guard looks away, as if some mark on the wall suddenly requires his undivided attention. He regrets speaking; everyone knows who Joe is, where he is from, and that he and the Commander are working on some grand plan for all of them. He is saved from further admonishments when two men arrive with a cart ladened with food. A pot of warm stew fills the area with its pleasant aroma, as does the smell of fresh bread, one of many innovations from Canfield.

"That was quick." Joe states, surprised by the speed at which they got the food and water.

"Yeah," One of the returning men replies, "the kitchen was putting this together when we arrived."

Joe's eyes narrow as he turns to look at Marco, questioningly.

"They looked hungry." Marco states bluntly as he returns Joe's gaze.

It suddenly dawns on Joe what has just transpired; Marco set this up so that the crew would learn to follow his instructions. He feels honored that Marco has so much faith and confidence in him.

Joe nods as he comprehends what this means for the future, then with a renewed confidence states, "Let these people out in small groups, for exercise and fresh air." He turns to one of the captives as he adds, "In time, these people will either join us, or leave us, but, whichever choice they make, it will be theirs!"

The captives shuffle as the words sink in, especially with one of the guards now being with them. One of the older captives looks to Joe, then pats his chest as he says, "I'm Pierre. You have my gratitude, and I speak for all of us when I say that we will not cause you any trouble."

Joe nods as he replies, "This crew is fair, but stern. If your people do as you say, they will treat you well. You have my word!"

Marco nods to the guards, adding, "I've been to Joe's domed city, and to the underground fortress, and I can tell you, we're lucky to have people like him on our side."

Pierre steps closer as he says, "Perhaps we're lucky that our engine blew! Our fleet is out of supplies. The Admiral ordered us to charge your fleet in the desperate hopes that you had food and fuel."

Joe freezes as the words sink in. He turns to Marco and says, "That fleet's going to attack Canfield!"

Marco turns and runs, sprinting toward the bridge, he shouts over his shoulder, "Not only is Canfield visible from the sea, that covered dock is a dead giveaway there are supplies nearby."

Pierre glances to his colleagues, then upon receiving their nods of approval, offers, "I might be able to help."

With Marco gone, his footfalls receding into the distance, it falls on Joe to decide what to do.

One of the guards straightens his shoulders, then says, "Your orders, Sir!"

Joe nods as he states, "Pierre will come with me." He pauses as he considers his position, then motioning to the guard Marco had tossed in with the captives, adding, "When your friend comes to his senses, let him out."

"Yes, Sir!" The guard replies with a grin.

Joe leads Pierre to the bridge, where they find Marco and Antonio deep in discussion with the other bridge officers.

"Sink 'em all!" Freddie states with conviction.

Paul cringes, mumbling, "We should just avoid 'em."

Antonio lifts his eyebrows when he sees Joe leading Pierre onto the bridge.

"I have an idea!" Pierre states, immediately getting everyone's undivided attention.

Antonio nods, as he replies, "Let's hear it."

Pierre takes a deep breath, then says, "I don't know how the Admiral's fleet is still afloat, but I do know that the crew's hungry, and the fuel cells are done for."

Antonio shrugs, "Tell me something I don't know."

Pierre glances around nervously, then states, "The crew's loyalty is to who can feed them. And you can."

"How could I trust such a crew?" Antonio questions, tilting his head as he waits for an answer.

"They just want to survive, and once they see your operation, they'll be swayed." Pierre replies.

Antonio narrows his eyes as he presses, "How can you be so sure?"

Pierre nods as he responds, "Because, I'd serve you."

Stroking the stubble on his chin, Antonio responds, "Only because we saved you from a sinking wreck?"

Pierre points to Joe as he says, "No, it's because you have people like him on your crew."

Joe glances back and forth, not sure what to say.

Antonio replies with a smile, "Joe is a good man!"

"Okay," Pierre continues, "if you can get me to the Admiral, I'm pretty sure I can get him to listen to you!"

"Well, let's hope we catch up to your fleet before they get to the coast, where they'll be destroyed." Antonio states bluntly.

"Destroyed?" Pierre queries.

"Yes!" Antonio states, then orders, "Make for Golem One, best possible speed. I want all lookouts doubled. No, tripled!"

The bridge crew relays the orders, then as Pierre watches, he realizes that this crew is not so different from his own. They are a little better fed, with a good ship under their feet, but, it is obvious that it has not always been this way. Every repair he has noticed has been recent, which means they found a safe place to refit and repair.

Joe turns to Pierre, and asks, "Did your fleet find any land which was safe?"

Pierre sighs as he replies, "We avoid the open ocean when we can, and hug the coast, looking for settlements to raid." He frowns and shakes his head as he continues, "But it was not always like that. Quite a few years ago we found a group of simple folk. They were on a small island just off the coast, quite a ways from here. There was no poisonous gas, and they grew their own food. We took what we wanted when we visited, but each time they had less and less, until the last time we went back." He stares directly into Joe's eyes as he finishes, "They were all dead."

"What did they die of?" Joe asks.

"It wasn't anything we did." Pierre hurriedly states, adding, "They weren't too bright. My guess is that something broke they couldn't fix. I don't know." He finishes with a shrug.

Antonio rubs his chin as he ponders the situation. He then says, "I think Kev was in contact with other fleets. It can't be a coincidence that your fleet is near ours, and you said that they're out of supplies." He looks arounds as he adds, "I bet that Kev was going to trade our surplus food for something from your fleet."

Pierre shrugs as he offers, "There were times we would leave caches on islands, or find 'em."

Marco nods, "Same here," He looks at Antonio as he adds, "but it's been a while since the last time we did either."

The Coast

Joe lowers his binoculars, then sighs as he hands them back to Marco. He shakes his head sorrowfully as the images of the shoreline remain embedded in his mind. He is quiet and sullen as he leaves the bridge, heading for a transport.

Antonio clenches his jaw as he states, "Fools!"

Thirty-seven ships line the shore, having beached themselves near the dock. The hulls on some of them were so weak, they caved in as the vessels ground into the shore, flooding the lower compartments and allowing the deadly mist to enter.

Canfield's dome is visible in the distance, rising above the mist like the ancient monolith it is. Bodies from those who succumbed to the gas line the shore, forming an arrow aimed at the dock. A few hapless survivors stand atop the decks of their beached ships, waving frantically. The gas is deceivingly thin on the shoreline, but still a deadly cocktail of corrosive chemicals.

Armed transports from Golem One begin arriving at the scene, and immediately set up a perimeter. There is nothing they can do for the dead, but those still alive may have a chance.

Henry contacts Dianne from the bridge, then before she can do more than identify herself, says, "I have to be quick. We found the base, and a few islands, where we could live, but, we also found a radio frequency we want to contact. It was on the wall of an old Luna launch facility."

"An old frequency?" Dianne queries, her curiosity mounting.

As Henry watches Golem's transports encircle the front of the beach vessels, he adds, "Don't kill the pirates, they might join us!"

Dianne begrudgingly replies, "I will order them to stay back, but, if they try anything, they will be killed."

"Understood." Henry replies, then cuts the communication.

A meaningful look passes between Henry, Jerry, Antonio, and Marco, then motioning for Pierre to follow them, they leave the bridge.

Freddie and Paul shrug as they watch the others leave, then issue orders to the fleet to hold fast, and wait.

Joe arrives at the rear of the old carrier, then stops when he sees the group before him.

Marco grins widely, "You didn't think we'd let you go alone? Did you?"

Antonio motions to Pierre as he says, "Here's your chance to convince the survivors to join us."

Henry walks over and slaps Joe on the back as he says, "Joe, you go and do what you're good at!"

"Me?" Joe replies with a confused frown, "I'm not really good at anything."

Jerry recalls the first time he saw Joe and smiles at the memory.

They step into an unarmed transport, then with Marco at the controls, make their way to the beach. Carefully navigating the debris piles, they arrive safely on the shore.

Cautiously, they approach the largest of the beached vessels, an ancient battleship. The battleship is truly a behemoth. Its rear floats in the water, while its bow is deeply embedded into the beach, having pushed the sand aside as it forced its way to shore. The vessel is eerily quiet, its engines silenced.

Pierre motions to the figures standing on the deck of the ship as he asks, "Is there any way we can speak to them?"

Marco nods, "The transport has a loudspeaker we can use, but unless they have a working radio, I doubt we'll be able to hear anything they say."

Antonio looks to Marco, who then switches on the speaker, and motions to a microphone.

Pierre leans in closer, takes a deep breath, then says, "This is Pierre! If you wish to live, you will join these people. I want you to meet someone, so stay put and don't do anything stupid." He glances through the windows at the line of beached ships, then adds, "Anything else stupid!"

Antonio frowns as he asks, "What do you have in mind?"

Pierre grins as he replies, "We all go to wherever you guys were going, then I go and speak to whoever is in charge of that old fleet, with Joe."

Joe groans as he replies, "Why me?"

Henry grins as he says, "Perfect! Let's roll."

Marco is sullen as he moves the transport up the beach toward the road, then accelerates toward Golem One. Driving past the bodies, numbering in the hundreds, they all silently wonder what would encourage them to make such a mad, and suicidal, dash for the dock.

Pierre shakes his head as he points, "Look! They were wearing some sort of makeshift facemasks made from what looks like scraps of clothing."

Jerry sighs as he replies, "They didn't know that the gas here is deadlier than on the ocean."

Pierre quietly mumbles, "More than half the crew."

Marco tilts his head as he questions, "What was your total compliment?"

"Before we engaged your fleet, we numbered around five hundred."

Antonio makes a mental count, including the ship they sank and the crew they saved, then says, "So, there's somewhere between one to two hundred survivors."

"Sounds about right." Pierre replies, nodding solemnly.

Jerry flicks a switch on his console, then speaks directly to the transports from Golem, "Jerry here. They're just desperate, given a chance they may join us. Contain them and wait for Dianne's orders."

Although Jerry is not in charge of the forces from Golem One, his standing with Dianne is well known, thus the force commander complies without a second thought.

Arriving at the coastal road, Marco wastes no time in getting the transport up to full speed as they rush toward Golem One.

Chapter Ten – Fateful Choices

Joe and Dianne walk along an upper terrace, one with an amazing view of the ocean, the beach, and both fleets. Fortunately, the bodies which line the shore from the beached vessels are too far away to be easily discerned.

Dianne waves to the chaotic scene as she asks, "What do we do about this?"

Joe sighs, then replies, "It wasn't that long ago I was walking along a street heading to work, in a city I thought had millions. I had no idea the world was in such a mess. I didn't know of this place, or the underwater facility. Any of it! And yet here we are, a handful of survivors from a forgotten war, all of us struggling to live."

"I don't want to kill them, but how can we trust them?" She states motioning to the stranded vessels.

"Pierre wants me to go with him to talk to them, besides, Antonio and Marco have more than proved themselves." Joe replies, "They can help too!"

Dianne's eyes narrow as she replies, "Proved themselves? Not really they haven't." She looks at Joe as she explains, "We repaired their ships, and they left. They haven't really had to do anything for us."

"They went to the islands you asked them to!" Joe counters. He recalls his trek across the ocean, then continues, "Besides, sailing with them these last few months has allowed me to get to know them pretty well."

"And you trust them?" She presses, still staring into his eyes.

"I do!" He states with conviction, then adds, "But, if you don't, you should do what you think is right."

She turns her attention back to the beach, then with a sigh, says, "We should give them a chance, like we did with Antonio's people."

Maggie runs up to them, interrupting their talk, then grabs both of their hands as she squeezes in between them. Looking up at Joe she giggles, "Welcome home!"

Joe stops, then frowns. He had never thought of Golem One as his home, but seeing her jubilant expression softens his as he replies, "Why thank you, young lady."

Dianne also stops as she gazes out across the ocean, the thin layer of deadly gas evident as far as the eye can see. She sighs as she asks, "Did you really find islands with animals?"

Joe's jaw drops as he recalls the numbers they found engraved into the wall. "We need to try to contact someone!" He blurts out.

Dianne's eyes sparkle energetically as she replies, "Relax, Henry's already on it."

"We need to be there!"

"We will be. The technicians have a little work to do in order to boost the signal strength." She gazes at him as she continues, "We wouldn't dream of contacting that number without you."

"Okay."

Maggie stays between them as she looks from her mother to Joe, then putting their hands together, she giggles as she skips happily away.

The pair stare at their interlocked hands for a moment before Dianne states, "Well, we know Maggie approves of you!"

Joe slowly releases her hand, then hesitantly asks, "Do you mind if I ask about her father?"

Dianne takes a deep breath, then folds her arms across her chest as she replies, "He was from Perkville, and not that I wish to speak ill of the dead, but he wasn't a good man. I'm not happy that he was killed in an explosion, but sometimes I feel as if it were some sort of poetic justice."

Joe lowers his gaze as he replies, "I'm sorry, I didn't mean to bring up bad memories. I don't know what I was thinking."

Dianne softens her gaze as she replies, "He wasn't a rough man, quite the contrary." She pauses as she tries to find the right words then says, "Let's just say, he had a way with the ladies, his way, and often! I didn't know this when he came here for a while."

Joe recalls what he knows of Perkville, then says, "They're the ones who make diesel engines, aren't they?"

"Yes, they are!" Dianne replies, adding, "And in case you're wondering, Maggie never met him. He left before she was born and died shortly after." She gazes into his eyes as she reaches for his hand, softly saying, "Until recently, I had no interest in anyone else."

Maggie saves Joe from any response when she comes running to them once more, this time squealing, "Mister Henry says he's almost ready. He told me to get you, quick!"

Dianne looks at Maggie, then flicks a glance to Joe as she smiles at his obvious awkwardness. She grabs his hand as she says, "C'mon!"

The three of them walk the short distance to the control room. Inside, they find Gordon and Henry enthusiastically engaged with a pair of technicians, with half a dozen others sitting back, watching.

Jerry stands patiently nearby, and nods to Dianne and Joe as they enter the room. He notices them holding hands, and smiles. In the beginning, he had watched Joe's interactions with Dianne carefully. His desire to protect her being his foremost concern. But his initial reservations have long since passed, and now he is happy that the two seem to be forming a relationship. His decision is helped by the fact that Maggie obviously likes Joe. Some had expected Jerry to become involved with Dianne, confusing his overt protectiveness of her as being more than his sworn duty, a task he happily performs.

One of the technicians, Michael, a younger man, is a fairly new addition to the tower's crew. He shakes his head as he states, "Even if that number is for the moon, there's no way anyone could have lived up there all this time."

"Why not?" Henry replies, repeating an ongoing debate between them all.

Dianne interrupts them when she states, "Well, let's find out shall we? Gentlemen!" She adds with mild sarcasm at their raised voices.

The second technician reviews his control panel, then motions as he says, "All we have to do is flick that switch, and talk. We've set up an open mic and fed the return signal to this panel's speakers." He finishes as he motions to the computer before him once more.

Dianne pauses, then says, "I guess you're waiting for me?"

Henry grins as he replies, "Well, it's your show!"

CLICK

The sound of the switch moving fills the silent room as everyone holds their breath, waiting.

Dianne takes a deep breath, breaking the silence, then says, "This is Dianne of Golem One, is anyone receiving me?"

There is no static, and no reply, nothing to indicate that they contacted anyone.

Dianne frowns as the seconds tick by, then says, "This is Golem One. Is anyone receiving this transmission?"

"Well, hello." The voice is deep and gravelly, and sounds unnatural.

"Who is this?" Dianne requests as she gazes around the room, her curiosity mounting.

"I have been watching you for some time and wondered if you would try to contact us." The speech is precise, and well measured.

"Where are you?" Dianne presses, wondering if the person replying is simply someone playing with them.

Sounds of people moving around and hushed whispers filter through the speakers, before finally another voice, a younger equally precise voice, responds. "I am overseer Volstrol. You have succeeded in contacting Moon Base Omega."

Dianne grins as she replies, "Yes, we discovered your message."

Volstrol chuckles as he replies, "The last of the ground teams abandoned the planet hundreds of years ago! There is no record of a message being left behind."

"This radio frequency was carved into the wall of a building my people found." Dianne explains.

"Ahh! That's how they did it." He replies, then adds, "Clever. They knew the computer systems wouldn't last."

"How many of you live up there?" She asks.

After a brief pause, Volstrol replies, "We have a sustained population of fifty thousand."

Gordon and Joe glance at each other, both instantly catching the man's interesting choice of words. Joe flicks a glance to Henry, then quietly moves toward Gordon, allowing them to briefly share their whispered thoughts.

Dianne's eyes narrow as she catches their brief exchanges, then presses on, "We have around two hundred fifty thousand people, spread out amongst various domes. Our Fleet Commander has been searching for somewhere where we could all live, safe, in the open!"

"Actually," Volstrol replies, "your world's population is closer to a million."

"A million!" Dianne exclaims.

"Yes. There are domes like yours all over the planet, and even a few smaller open-air communities."

"You can see all this?" Dianne asks, stunned at the idea.

Gordon, Henry and Joe nod to each other. They had been discussing the likelihood that there would be others.

Volstrol's voice resounds from the speakers once more, "Your best option is to head south. The southern parts of the world suffered less, and thus have recovered faster."

"You should visit us." Dianne offers, looking around at the others as she shrugs.

"We do not have the need or desire go planet-side!" Volstrol states bluntly.

Dianne hesitates as she considers the various reports, then replies, "What if we were able to repair the launch facilities, and come and visit you?"

Volstrol is clearly uncomfortable as he replies, "But, but why would you do that? We are thriving, and you will too, in time. You have no need to come here." His measured voice and tone losing some of its control.

Henry gets Dianne's attention, then at her approving nod, says, "This is Henry, from Canfield." He pauses, but when there is no response, he continues, "I imagine that your facilities are somewhat limited, and over time, you have adapted to the lower gravity, and like us, filtered light. You could leave the confines you live in and join us."

Volstrol replies indignantly, "Our facilities are not limiting our populace, they accommodate them well. We have few sicknesses or diseases, thanks to our advancements in the medical field, and have no desire to expose ourselves to the planet's environment."

Henry glances to Dianne, shakes his head, then replies, "This is why you do not want us to visit you!"

Volstrol replies a moment later, "You would bring disease and chaos with you. Our society is well balanced. We will not let you interfere with the order of things."

Henry frowns at his choice of words, pausing as he deliberates over his reply.

Joe feels a chill run up his spine at the realization that Volstrol sounds exactly like the Central Authority from Canfield. He leans toward Dianne and whispers in her ear, "He's afraid!"

Dianne's confident voice fills the air, "Canfield was just like you not too long ago…"

"No one is like us!" Volstrol rudely interrupts, adding proudly "We are one hundred percent self-sustaining!"

Henry's eyes narrow as he replies, "But you can't expand, can you? You're at the limits of your facility's capabilities."

Hushed whispers, and chaotic voices resonate from the speakers, their only reply.

Dianne offers, "We could help each other, for the sake of all of us."

They strain to hear what is happening on the moon base. It is clear that there is some sort of debate raging about how best to protect themselves, then the speakers go eerily quiet.

Joe picks up a few fragmented words, then feels another chill run up his spine as a thought races through his mind. He lunges for the switch, flicks it off, then fearfully states, "I heard attack!"

Dianne immediately orders, "Enable full protection protocol!" She did not hear anything about an attack, but trusts Joe implicitly.

Henry also failed to hear anything that would suggest an attack, and frowns in confusion as he watches thick protective slabs slide over the windows, then feels the entire tower sinking into the mountain top. Elsewhere throughout Golem One, massive slabs of concrete seal them off from the outside, entombing them.

Gordon looks at Henry, then Joe. His eyes narrow as he says, "I didn't catch anything about an attack."

Joe shakes as he wonders if he misheard, then says, "They were discussing ways to protect themselves from us."

Jerry's jaw drops as he questions, "Why would they attack?"

BOOM

The explosion rocks the facility. The lights flicker as flecks of concrete and dust fall from the ceiling. The computers remain on, their power coming from a different circuit.

Other, more distant explosions can be heard, but as for where the impacts are, no one knows for sure.

Dianne feels a rage building in her like never before, "Why?" She screeches.

Jerry points to a massive spike on a radiation meter, then stares stoically ahead as he states, "It's us or them!"

BOOM

Another massive explosion rocks the facility, showering them with more dust. A huge chunk of concrete unexpectedly falls from the corner and hits the floor with a resounding thud. The nuclear blast wave is more powerful than the first and shakes the tower in its unrelenting fury.

Emotion overtakes Dianne as she realizes that the people outside are dying, all because of her! Her lips quiver as she makes a fateful decision. "Prepare to set coordinates for all weapons. We need to find the location of that base!"

Henry shakes the dust off his head as he asks, "What about the pre-war maps?"

The computer operators immediately bring up their records. One of them points to his screen, exclaiming as he does so. "Oh, my!"

Dianne reads the information quickly, then frowns as she reviews the detailed maps and plans. Her face quivers as emotions boil over. "These records show that Canfield, Golem One, and half a dozen other cities built the moon base! How did we not see this before?"

Joe's jaw drops as he states, "So we were all on the same side, once!"

Dianne points to an area on the moon, then confidently states, "There!"

Joe stares at the screen, then questions, "That's not the main dome?"

"I doubt our weapons could damage their dome, much like theirs aren't getting through our protection."

Henry leans forward then says, "That's their aquafer, isn't it? It's pretty deep."

"We only have to contaminate it, to make them stop. They'll have to listen to us then." Dianne explains.

Joe nods as he adds his thoughts, "Just like when Aqua stopped producing water, it forced us to work together."

BOOM

The explosion is more powerful than the others. It knocks them off their feet and cuts the power, leaving them staring into the darkness, suddenly afraid. They breathe a sigh of relief when the lights flicker back on. Their relief is short lived. Huge cracks in the ceiling make it look more like shattered glass than the smooth concrete of before.

Dianne orders, "As soon as those computers cycle up, fire everything we have at those coordinates, then abandon the tower, I doubt it can take much more."

They all watch the expanding cracks in the failing ceiling as they nervously wait while the consoles power back up. As soon as they are able, the operators hurriedly program the missiles with their new target coordinates, then look to Dianne. At her nod, they engage the launch sequences, then stand, their task is done.

Joe frowns as he asks, "It's that easy? You don't have some special codes, or safety protocols to follow?"

Dianne nods sadly, replying, "Yes, it's that easy to kill thousands, upon thousands of people."

Joe swallows hard as he hurriedly replies, "That's not what I meant by easy."

Dianne takes his hand as she says, "I know what you meant. I just want everyone to understand what the consequences of our actions are."

A distorted and crackled voice comes from the speakers, "We didn't mean to launch! It was the automatics. We tried to override the system…" Volstrol's voice cuts out, whether by choice or not, they do not know.

Dianne numbly states, "Even if we believe him, we can't stop the missiles now."

Joe's jaw drops as he states more than asks, "You don't have some sort of self-destruct mechanism?"

She shakes her head sorrowfully, her only reply.

Michael stares at his console, then alarms everyone when he shouts, "Oh no! We must reverse the air. We need Aqua to switch from receiving to sending."

Dianne stares fearfully as she replies, "Do it!" She is relieved beyond all measure that they had Aqua's oxygenators repaired, otherwise, their fate would be sealed.

Michael sends messages, then works frantically with operators in Aqua to get the air systems reversed, all the while, aware of the expanding cracks in the ceiling.

Apocalypse

Missiles rise from hidden bunkers all over the mountain, dozens of them. They climb majestically on pillars of smoke and fire as they rocket upward, passing others in the sky which rain down from the moon base, until both facilities have fully exhausted their supplies.

BOOM!

The impact shakes the tower, showering them with more debris. The lights flicker, then go out, and stay out.

Jerry turns on his flash light, points it at a door as he shouts, "There!"

Gordon rushes for the door. Holding it open, he squints into the darkness.

"Maggie!" Dianne shouts as she peers into the darkness, her heart beating quickly as her fear builds.

"Mom, I'm here." Maggie replies, scurrying out from between a chair and a computer console.

Dianne grabs her hand, then joins the others as they hurry for the stairwell. Flashlights stab through the haze as they flee down the stairs. There is no central core to peer down as they zig zag back and forth. They have no idea where the bottom is, until they reach a solid door. The door has not been used in a long time and is wedged shut.

Jerry slams into the door over and over, until it finally moves. Light and fingers poke through the opening from the other side and pull, aiding their efforts. Once open, they spill out into Golem's main cavern, which still has power along with hundreds of people.

Some of those in the cavern are staring at the ceiling with numbed expressions, others rush about in a panic, while a few are attempting to push past the guards who stand before the closed ramp.

Between deep breaths Jerry motions to the door they forced open, and states, "We have to shut that door, now!"

"Did everyone get out?" Dianne asks as she glances around, counting.

Michael coughs as he replies, "Yes, I made sure of it."

Pierre runs to the group, then fearfully asks, "What's going on?"

Dianne shakes her head at the interruption as she replies, "They launched weapons at us, but it may have been some dreadful mistake."

"Who launched?" Pierre demands, fear in his eyes.

Joe walks to Pierre, then puts a hand on his shoulder as he explains, "The moon base launched missiles at us, but as Dianne said, it may not have been intentional." He flicks a glance to Dianne, before returning his attention back to Pierre.

"How the hell do you shoot at someone by mistake?" Pierre demands, waving his arms in frustration.

Joe reflects on their own missiles being fired, and replies, "Computers make it too easy."

Dianne cringes at the slight barb, flicking an annoyed glance to Joe. She did not have time to decide what to do and acted to protect them all.

"I need to see to the lads!" Pierre presses, stepping away from Joe he starts to walk toward the closed ramp, where the guards are having trouble holding back the growing crowd.

Someone starts a transport vehicle and recklessly accelerates toward the ramp, and its sealed doorway. People scatter in all directions as the vehicle plows through them, striking those too slow to get out of its way. The vehicle is still accelerating when it slams into the steel and concrete barricade which blocks the passageway. Its front end is crushed as it stops abruptly. Momentum carries the unrestrained driver forward, slamming him into the vehicle's controls, shattering his ribs and face. He takes a few shuddering breaths, then dies. Injured people crawl away from the scene as the guards do their best to keep the crowd under control. The noise in the cavern is deafening as people scream and shout.

Jerry strides to catch up to Pierre and stops him, saying, "They're dead! Radiation counters are off the scale. Nothing can survive that."

The sound of the tower's roof caving in and crashing down on the elevator gets everyone's attention. All eyes stare fearfully upward at the ceiling overhead. Massive lights swing back and forth on the long cables as the rock above is pummeled over and over again by powerful explosions.

"Secure that!" Jerry shouts as dust falls from the gaps between the bottom of the elevator and the walls.

A group of men and women rush to the elevator where they climb ladders on either side of the lift mechanism. Reaching the underside of the ramp, they struggle to slide huge steel bars along old grooves beneath the elevator, even as it shudders and threatens to fall. The bars will prevent the elevator from falling, but they do not stop the steady stream of dust.

Jerry turns back to Pierre, wondering what to do with the man, then says, "If you want to stay safe, help them and go where they go."

Pierre looks around fretfully, then nods. He is glad to have a task to keep his mind off the loss of his friends. He strides with purpose to the elevator, then skillfully climbs a ladder, where he adds his efforts to securing it.

A guard hurries to Dianne then, without a word, shows her his radiation meter. It is climbing. The dust which falls around the elevator is heavily contaminated.

Dianne shouts, ordering, "Abandon the main dock! Take everything you can, we'll be sealing this area off in thirty minutes!"

Voices cry out that they must get out before they all die.

Dianne shouts over the din as loudly as she can, "Even if you could survive the gas, radiation levels are lethal outside. We have another way. Follow me!"

Joe smiles as he asks, "We have another way out?"

Dianne stares at him for a moment before replying flatly, "No!"

Maggie hugs Dianne as she stares wide-eyed at the swinging lights, a few of which have failed, casting great swathes of gloomy patches on the floor.

Pete rushes toward Dianne, then as he takes a deep breath, reports, "I'll secure the rest of the transports!"

Dianne nods as she states, "Don't get trapped. We're sealing the dock!"

"I won't. See you below." He replies, then rushes off.

High overhead, dozens of fiery plumes rise from the earth, each carrying vast amounts of debris up from the ground. The fleet on the beach is hit by a direct impact, and instantly vaporized, leaving no survivors. Antonio's fleet fares no better, with each of the ships being no match for the powerful nuclear blasts. The carrier is the last to sink, taking with it their hopes of finding a new home. The crew had ordered the fleet to flee the moment they saw the first explosion over Golem One, but their ships were no match for the fury of the blasts. The attack does not last long, but its wrath changes the landscape, forever. The rising plumes of radioactive dust block out the sun, with the shockwaves themselves creating huge tsunamis which travel a third of the way around the world.

Beneath Golem One

Joe is astounded as they trek downward into the depths of the earth. He had thought the upper areas of Golem One were the bulk of the facility, but he could not have been more wrong. Three large tunnels lead from the main chamber, each now sealed shut, downward to a world he had never imagined. He is further surprised when Dianne leads them to an electric tram.

Maggie holds Dianne's hand as the pair steps aboard, ahead of the computer operators from the tower, including Michael. Joe follows, then Gordon, Henry, Jerry, Antonio, and Marco, all of whom find seats. Pete is still moving every transport he can into the safety of the depths and plans to join them later.

Dianne sits near the tram's driver. She smiles approvingly as Joe sits next to Maggie, who is staring vacantly out the large window, events overwhelming her. Although she has the window seat, they both have a commanding view as they begin to leave the station.

Dianne states confidently, "As long as we get fresh water from Aqua, we can survive down here, indefinitely."

The tram passes vast caverns filled with plants, farmland, and even parks, which radiate out in all directions from a central core. The deeper they go, the warmer it gets as they pass vast estates packed with apartment buildings, followed by massive industrial complexes for as far as the eye can see. Yet still they travel deeper into the earth's crust.

Joe's jaw drops when they arrive at a station, complete with four tracks alongside two platforms, two with trams, sitting, waiting.

Dianne motions upward as she proudly states, "We lost the tower and the dock, but not Golem One itself!" She stands, then exits the tram and waits on the platform for the others.

"What about the air? Surely its contaminated!" Joe states more than asks, his voice quivering a little as he leads Maggie to the platform.

Dianne smiles as she replies, "We have air purification centers. But," she adds hesitantly, "they require vast amounts of water, which is why Aqua is so important to us, especially now."

Jerry nods solemnly as he adds, "We had just started drawing air in from the upper tower too, but we can't do that anymore."

Henry frowns as he looks around, "You almost have a closed system, but not quite. It makes me wonder how they did it on the moon."

Michael turns around and hesitantly says, "The aquafer we targeted was only one of two systems. I noticed the second after we launched, but anyway, that one system alone held over a trillion liters of water."

"A trillion liters each!" Joe stammers, adding, "Where'd they get all that water from?"

Henry feels a chill run up his spine as he answers, "I wonder if that's what started the war."

Jerry shakes his head doubtingly but says nothing.

"No listen." Henry presses, catching Jerry's expression. He explains, "We've been told all along that the world was running out of resources. Well, with the moon taking, what, two trillion liters?

Maybe even more, I bet people down here became concerned."

Jerry replies, "That's not really a lot of water, not in the great scheme of things."

Joe offers, "It would be if the world's waterways were becoming polluted." He glances around, adding, "That much fresh, clean water, it had to come from somewhere."

Gordon motions to Henry and Joe as he says, "You could be right!"

Dianne frowns as she shares her thoughts, "That moon base was not only self-sufficient, they had weapons!"

Gordon recalls what he knows, then suggests, "I think Canfield, along with a bunch of other facilities were built before the war as..."

Joe interrupts him, stammering, "Oh my! As a pilot test project."

Henry agrees with the pair, adding, "A feasibility study."

Dianne's jaw drops as she says, "And we were spared the worst of the initial attacks, because we were on the same side."

Gordon looks around as he says, "We're still missing a lot of information, but it does appear that our side did win."

Antonio, who has been quietly listening, until now, snorts, "Some victory! You were forced to live in domes or underground."

Dianne sighs as she states, "Well, this debate, though interesting, has to wait. We need to contact Aqua."

Henry nods in agreement as he says, "Along with Canfield, and the other communities."

"This way!" Dianne motions as she reaches for Maggie's hand.

The entire entourage walks toward a large building where two guards stand before a pair of massive doors. The guards glance to each other, then recognizing Dianne, Maggie, and Jerry, they open the doors, revealing a huge chamber.

Following Dianne inside, Joe immediately notices the central stage, which houses a long table, where a few people are seated. Looking around he sees that three sides of the room are dominated by hundreds of empty elevated seats, like theater seating.

Dianne turns and says, "I hate politics, but it's the way things are, so here goes."

Five people are seated at the table; three men and two women. Four of them stand as Dianne strides in, hand in hand with Maggie, with everyone else trailing behind. The five people are all wearing colorful robes, some of them with fine embroidery evident on them.

One of those standing, a bald, old man, whose deep-red robe is by far the most glamorous, demands, "You dare interrupt a council meeting!"

Dianne flicks a glance to the group, then pauses at Joe as she nods her head toward Maggie. Joe understands the gesture and takes Maggie's hand, then stops and waits with the others. The group stands well back from the council members, but close enough to hear all that is said. Gordon, Henry, and Joe, quietly discuss their survival options, quickly sorting out their wants and needs.

Dianne continues toward the table as a handful of guards stride out to block her. She tilts her head at them and waves her hand dismissively as she steps closer. The guards look from her to the council, then, without a word, step away, allowing her to pass.

The bald man stammers, "Stop her!"

Dianne reaches the table, leans on it, then says, "Shut up and listen for once in your miserable life!"

The others at the table gasp in disbelief, while a couple of the guards stifle chuckles.

She continues, "Unless you're stupid, you have to know by now that the tower and dock are lost to us."

The bald man shakes with anger as he shouts, "You will address me as Chairman Lee!" Flecks of spittle strike the table as he struggles to contain his anger.

Dianne sits on the edge of the table, then leaning closer says, "Very well. Chairman Lee! The tower and main dock are lost."

Lee points a bony finger at Dianne as he demands, "How can you lose them? They're impenetrable!"

Dianne shakes her head in disbelief as she replies, "You really don't know, do you?"

Lee looks at the others as he shrugs, "We heard a few ridiculous, wild, exaggerated stories of being under attack."

Dianne pokes his chest as she states, "If you got off your scrawny ass and looked, you'd know."

Lee's jaw drops as he squeals, "She touched me! That's a violation of Council Law!"

Another lady, Heather, stands, then condescendingly says, "Dianne, I understand that you've been under a lot of stress lately, perhaps…"

"Stress!" Joe interrupts loudly, "You want to see stress. Go outside!"

"Remove him!" Lee demands with a wave of his hand. "Remove them all!"

Jerry steps forward as he states, "Remove yourself."

Lee stammers wide-eyed as he stares at the non-moving guards. "I gave you an order!" he screeches; more spittle flies from his mouth as he rages.

Dianne sighs as she gets off the table, then begins pacing before them, saying, "The moon base attacked us with nuclear weapons. Even as we speak, radiation is seeping into the main dock, and unless we act, will eventually make its way down, perhaps even reaching here."

Lee's eyes narrow as he spitefully states, "That dock has held for hundreds of years! You have failed in your task, Dianne! I cast a vote of no confidence in you." He looks to the others at the table as he demands, "Your votes?"

Heather nods, and with a devilish grin, states, "I agree."

The man and woman next to her hesitate, they have met Dianne and come to know her. They disagree, leaving the last person, a wrinkled old man who has seen more years than most, to cast his vote. He stands, slowly and painfully.

Shaking unsteadily on his feet, Zack's body is bent with age, as are his fingers from arthritis. His robe is spartan, compared to the others, its blue hue is faded from wear. He holds onto the table, his cobalt eyes blazing with energy as he states, "I have seen many things, even the outside," he waves to Dianne as he explains, "That was long before you were born, young lady." He breaths steadily as he continues, "I nominated you for the position you have, and still stand by that decision."

Lee is furious. Shaking his fist at Zack he demands, "You should have died long ago, old man."

Zack straightens as much as he can, then staring directly into Lee's eyes states, "You always were a coward, and lazy."

Lee steps to Zack then pushes him back into his chair as he states, "I do not recognize your vote, old man!"

The lady who voted with Zack smiles. It is the smile of a predator that is about to strike. She has waited many years for an opportunity such as this as she states, "Lee, you don't respect the laws of this Council, and yet you expect others to. I vote for your removal, and for Zack's reinstatement as Chairman."

Lee folds his arms triumphantly as Heather votes for him to remain, then his face goes slack as the others vote against him.

Zack slowly rises to his feet, then says, "I accept the nomination and immediately appoint Dianne to the task of resolving our situation."

Lee stammers, then turning to Heather states, "We should leave this farce immediately." He turns to leave, then hesitates when Heather sits down, and watches as she turns to Zack and nods respectfully.

Heather has been on the council much of her life and knows how to play the political field well. She coughs lightly, then says, "It seems I was ill informed by Chairman Lee as to the dire nature of our situation," She casts Lee a scathing glance, then continues, "I suggest that Dianne be offered our full support, along with whatever resources she and her team requires, in this endeavor."

Dianne nods slowly, then says, "We must contact Aqua, Canfield, Perkville, and the other outlying communities to determine their status."

Lee storms off squealing, "You've not heard the end of this. You'll see!"

Zack sits down, his bones creaking louder than his chair, as he says, "Dianne, the last time you came here you talked of expanding the council. What happened?" He then interrupts himself, stating, "How rude of me. Introductions are in order."

"First," Dianne presses, "we need to contact the other communities."

Michael nudges his counterpart, saying, "We got this. Just tell us where your communications room is."

One of the council guards glances to Zack, then upon receiving his nod of approval, states, "Come with me."

Zack lifts his eyebrows as he questions, "Now, introductions! I'm Zack." He then motions along the table to the others as he continues, "Heather, Scott, Stephanie, and the man who left, is Lee." He motions to the group as he asks, "And your friends are?"

As the trio leaves, Dianne rattles off everyone's name, then smiles thinly. Without further ado, she relays the events of the last few months. Joe, along with the others, fill in their experiences of the trek to the islands, the hostile fleet, then Dianne ends with the fateful communication to the moon base.

Heather taps her fingers on the table as she states, "Such a high-level communication between us and the moon, should have been approved first. Look where it got us!"

Zack leans back in his chair, then after a moments silence, states, "If Dianne had to ask us for advice every time there was a decision, she wouldn't be deserving of her position."

Scott and Stephanie, the pair who travelled to the tower when Aqua was damaged, nod in agreement. Heather looks around, with Lee gone, she suddenly feels quite alone as she stammers, "I was just saying!"

Dianne walks toward Heather, then narrows her eyes as she taunts, "It's easy to sit down here, safe, and make decisions. When was the last time you went to the surface, and actually looked for yourself instead of sending others?"

Heather sneers, "Well, thanks to you, I can't now, can I?"

"How convenient for you!" Dianne hisses, her eyes narrowing like a predator about to strike.

Zack raps the table with his walking stick as he states, "Ladies! Ladies!"

Scott casts his gaze up and down the table, then says, "Our council is too small, and has been for a long time. We had previously passed a vote to expand the council, and I see no reason to delay."

Heather stands as she says, "I shall get Councilman Lee."

Zack smiles softly, a smile which alarms Heather more than any other expression could have. She stops in her tracks as he states, "Lee is no longer a council member. He forfeited his right to a seat when he failed to request a vote for one. Instead, he chose to leave."

Scott chuckles loudly, "In his fit of rage, he assumed he'd still have a seat, but that's not how it works!"

Heather holds her head high as she states, "For a council seat, I nominate…" She looks around at the others, then surprises almost everyone when she coolly announces, "Dianne!"

Zack nods as he replies, "Well played!"

Scott and Stephanie add their positive votes, then turn to Zack.

Dianne frowns as she looks up and down the table at the council members, then asks, "Heather? I don't get it? I thought you didn't like me."

Before she can reply, Zack explains, "As your nominator, Heather automatically has your vote when you're absent from meetings."

Heather grins wolfishly as she says, "And I expect that with your duties, you will be very, very, busy, my dear."

Dianne swallows hard as she mumbles, "I hate politics."

Joe frowns as he watches the events play out. He stares at Zack, then blinks suddenly when the old man winks at him. His frown deepens as he realizes that Zack wanted Heather to nominate Dianne, but as for why, he has no idea.

"They're alive!" Michael shouts as he rushes into the chamber, interrupting them.

"Who's alive?" Dianne questions, wondering who they managed to contact.

"Everyone!" Michael replies excitedly.

Zack stands unsteadily as he announces, "As chairman, I conscript Heather to taking Dianne, and her entourage, to secured living, so that they may work on a plan to save us all."

Heather's jaw drops as she realizes that she has little recourse but to do as requested. She offers a thin smile as she stands and replies, "As you wish."

Joe looks at Zack, then smiles as the old man offers a slight nod. As they leave, Zack's voice resounds loudly as he nominates people for the council, along with his suggestion of expanding Dianne's powers.

Heather casts a hate filled glance back at Zack, then puts on a fake smile as she says with exaggerated flair, "This way, please."

The Villa

The group follows Heather to the trams, then boards a different one than the one they arrived in. This tram takes them through a long tunnel, then exits into a massive, well-lit, chamber. A pair of tracks seem to climb the walls as they curve around the inside edge of the enormous cavern, offering them a panoramic view as they climb higher and higher. The cavern's center is dominated by a park, complete with a sparkling lake in its midst. Apartment-style complexes line the edge of the park, while pedestrians walk along the pathways between each building.

Joe's jaw drops when he notices where they are going. He stammers, "Will you look at that!"

The tram passes between a pair of massive gates, and into a complex nestled into the side of the cavern. Huge walls, lined with guards, stand on either side of the tracks. Once the tram passes through, a pair of massive gates slide together, interlocking solidly. The tram stops at a platform, with another waiting on the other side.

Henry whistles as he exclaims, "The energy requirements for all of this must be huge!"

Heather momentarily forgets who she is with as she shrugs, replying, "The workers do all that stuff. We don't have to worry about it."

Dianne shakes her head in disgust but remains quiet. She grips Maggie's hand a little tighter as they walk along a stone-paved courtyard, lined with massive pots with small trees growing in them. She studies the older woman as she and the others follow.

Every step Heather takes strikes the ground with a sharp and forceful impact, which jostles the golden robe she wears. She walks with her head held high, as if to garner attention and to show everyone how important she is. To most, her jerky walk makes her look like a bird as she struts along, while Jerry likens her to a soldier marching in a parade. Although she is putting a lot of vigor into her pace, she actually moves quite slowly.

Joe takes advantage of the slow pace and looks up at the ceiling where banks of powerful lights radiate evenly. He motions to Gordon as he says, "It's like being outside on a cloudy day." He stops at the idea of the analogy, then smiles. He was thinking of Canfield, then realizes that he has been outside, unlike most people, and has truly experienced a cloudy sky.

Gordon stops as he looks upward, then lifts his eyebrows as he wonders if Joe is losing his mind. He casts his gaze around at the majestic stone buildings which line the sides of the courtyard and says, "It *is* just like being outside!"

Heather puts her hands on her hips, then with a deep sigh states, "I have no idea what you two are talking about. Now, if you want to get to your quarters, you will follow me."

Dianne purses her lips, but once more remains quiet. Heather is the slowest of them all.

Arriving at the end of the courtyard, they are greeted by a handful of men and women, all dressed in plain-grey garb. The workers stand on the steps which lead to an impressive stone building. Dozens of windows face them from the three-story structure, each with ornate carvings on either side.

Heather turns and says, "We don't get guests here, anymore, so I will order the house staff to figure that out." She snaps her fingers authoritatively as she dictates, "Rooms for these… visitors." She finishes, then without another word she turns to leave.

Dianne stares at Heather in disbelief, then finally has had enough. She bluntly states, "You're not special! You're the same as everybody else. What gives you the right to talk to these people like that?"

Heather stares at Dianne contemptuously, then states, "You would do well to watch your manners. I could have assigned you workers' quarters!" She strides off before anyone can reply, then turning back, she sneers, "Zack won't live much longer, which means you won't be staying here long!"

They all watch as Heather walks away, her forceful stride jerking her head with each stomp.

One of the plainly dressed women steps forward, curtsies, then with head held low timidly requests, "Please, come with me. There are plenty of rooms to choose from."

Dianne scowls, "You don't have to kowtow to me, and if I have any say to the matter, you won't to her either."

"Yes ma'am," The lady replies, then hesitantly adds, "but… she is on the council."

Joe steps forward, and with a wide grin states, "And so is Dianne!"

The group of workers mumble to themselves, surprised that Heather did not mention that fact to them.

Dianne reaches out to the lady, and with a smile asks, "What's your name?"

The lady hesitates for a moment, then replies, "Rebecca. My name is Rebecca, and I am responsible for this villa."

"This villa?" Dianne questions as she looks at the majestic building.

"Yes," Rebecca replies politely, adding, "each council member has their own villa, with this one being assigned for guests."

Dianne smiles as she replies, "You must get a lot of guests."

Joe turns and studies the courtyard, where he now notices eight other villas, four per side, each one seemingly carved into the stone walls. A few workers come and go from each of the buildings, with those in front of one building, working at a feverish pace as Heather approaches, where she enters as if she were royalty.

Rebecca shuffles nervously as she replies, "You're the first visitors I have ever seen."

An old lady shuffles forward; her head and hands shake unsteadily, as if from some motor-neuron disorder. Her eyes are covered in a grey film, which hinders her vision. With a croaky voice she says, "I remember a time when we used to have visitors. It was long ago, and I was but a little girl. My mother used to work for the council..."

Rebecca chastises, "Clarice! We've all heard your stories, now please go and clean something."

Dianne smiles warmly, then says, "Rebecca, I haven't heard the stories."

Rebecca takes a deep breath, sighs, then rolls her eyes as she motions to the old lady, saying, "Go on then."

Clarice shuffles to the side, then sits on the steps. She licks her wet lips, and begins, "Zack was a young man once. We used to go on adventures together. He took me to underwater cities, and others covered in huge domes."

While she talks, Joe feels a chill run up and down his spine. He quietly steps to Gordon and whispers, "She said underwater cities. Plural!"

Gordon looks at Joe in surprise as he whispers back, "I missed that, but you're right."

Joe motions to Jerry and Henry to join them, and while the old lady talks, they follow her story, trying to see how it relates to their current situation. Dianne listens intently as well, then glances to Rebecca, alarmed, as Clarice closes her eyes and her words become slurred. A moment later Clarice slumps over, her head lolling on her chest. Drool spills from the corner of her open mouth as she snores lightly.

Rebecca purses her lips as two strong workers gently lift the sleeping woman and carry her off.

Maggie surprises everyone with her young voice as she asks, "Is she okay?"

Rebecca glances to Dianne, momentarily alarmed, then shakes her head as she pauses, considering her words. She takes a deep breath, then looking at Maggie, replies, "She is old and senile, and..." She stops when she realizes she is about to repeat Heather's harsh words. She glances to the retreating trio, then instead simply says, "We care for her as best we can."

Joe approaches Dianne, nods, then looks to Rebecca as he requests, "Is there a communications room we could use?"

"Yes." She replies, happy to be changing the subject. She waves her arms at the villas as she adds, "Each has its own meeting room, complete with a computer terminal."

Dianne smiles warmly as she asks, "Could you please take us there?"

Rebecca looks at the large group, then cringingly replies, "The room will need to be prepared. Also, it's too small for all of you, perhaps I could take you to your rooms, then half a dozen of you could go to the meeting room once it's ready." She shrugs as she adds, "That's all the seats it has."

"Okay, let's do that then." Dianne concedes.

Rebecca leads them to the uppermost level, where she motions to rooms with either one or two beds in each. It takes a while to situate everyone, by which time Rebecca is pressing them to eat.

Another delay! But they have not eaten since morning and have no idea when their next meal will be.

Dianne looks up from her emptied plate, surprised by how hungry she was. She has been considering who should be in the communications room, then says, "Joe, Gordon, Henry, Jerry, Antonio, and Michael should join me in the meeting room."

Marco notices his name is absent, then hurriedly asks, "Can I come too?" He looks around then offers, "I'm sure it's standing room only, but I don't mind. I just want to be involved."

Dianne smiles as she replies, "Well, I miscounted already, so what's one more?"

Maggie tugs at Dianne's sleeve, then looks at her with desperate, pleading eyes. She does not want to be separated from her.

Dianne looks at Maggie, then smiles softly as she says, "I wouldn't dream of not taking you!"

Joe casts his gaze around the room, then nods to Dianne as he states, "We're all in this together; it's only right we all go."

Chapter Eleven – Survival

The room is crowded, but it is not as small as they had expected. They gather around a single small terminal, and wait, patiently. Michael sits at the controls, with Dianne and Maggie seated next to Joe, Henry, and Gordon. Extra seats are brought in for Antonio, Marco, and Jerry.

Dianne glances around at the group, then offers a thin smile as she says, "Let's find out how bad it is out there."

Michael flicks a switch, then says, "This is Golem One, calling Aqua."

The reply is almost instant, and crystal clear, "This is Ken from Aqua, we've been waiting for you."

Dianne leans toward the console, where the microphone is, and says, "Ken, Dianne here. How are things? Just a quick summary."

Ken pauses as stares at the list he has created, then realizing that it all comes down to one thing. He puts his list down and replies, his voice coming through load and clear, "Power, water, and air transfer lines are intact, as are communications, obviously. But, radiation levels are deadly on the surface as well as…" he pauses again, before slowly adding, "as well as around the ships which sank."

Antonio hopes his fleet was too far away to be affected. He looks around, not wanting to interrupt, but also desperate to find out how many survived.

Dianne catches his expression and says, "If any of you have questions, now is the time! Speak up."

Antonio blurts out, "How many ships sank?"

The room goes quiet as they wait for a reply.

After what feels like an eternity, Ken states, "Our drones saw none on the surface." He quickly adds, "But the radiation renders the drones useless pretty quickly…" His voice trails off as he realizes that he is offering false hopes. Even if any ships are still afloat, their crews would surely be dead.

Antonio is not sure if he is angry or sad; his emotions threaten to overcome him. Marco is stunned by the revelation that their shipmates are dead. While they all expected the beached crews to have perished, none had thought that the refitted fleet would meet the same fate.

Dianne frowns as she asks, "You mentioned radiation levels around the sunken ships. Is that an issue?"

"We're still running tests and evaluating the long-term effects." Ken replies. He hesitates once more as he tries to find the right words. Then, with a sigh, he states, "Initial analysis indicates that this facility will be rendered inhospitable in six months, with our water supplies being too contaminated to utilize in less than half that time."

"Six months!"

"Between the surface radiation sinking, and the ocean currents spreading it from the wrecks, we're in trouble." Ken explains, adding, "We're evaluating other routes for the pipelines, which, if successful, should provide us clean water for a few more months. But beyond that, it's pointless, this facility will be too heavily contaminated."

Dianne puts a hand to her mouth as she takes in the news, then says, "We must build massive storage tanks, here in Golem One. That will buy us some time."

"It won't help much."

She leans back in her chair as it dawns on her that the real issue is not the water. With a sigh she says, "It's the oxygenators. Isn't it?"

"Yes," Ken replies, adding, "the scrubbers are only able to filter out so much radiation before the filtration unit itself becomes contaminated."

Antonio glances around, confused, then asks, "Why not just move the facility?"

Ken's reply is almost instant, "That was our first thought as well, but the real issue is that the pipelines would still become irradiated."

Gordon adds his voice when he asks, "Couldn't we bury the pipes?"

"You're talking about relocating this entire facility as well as tunneling for new pipework. All in a matter of months!" Ken replies.

Joe glances to Gordon, then asks, "If, and I mean if, you got the resources you needed. Could it be done?"

Ken's chuckle comes through the room's speakers as he says, "Anything is possible, *if* we have enough resources."

Dianne nods as she says, "Then, Ken, it looks like we have a plan!"

Ken feels a chill run up his spine. He is not afraid, it is more of a chill of excitement as what he thought were impossibilities, may actually be possible. He replies, "I will meet with the engineers here, and see what they say."

"Good," Dianne replies, adding, "We have to contact Canfield, Perkville, as well as the other outlying communities."

"Understood. Aqua out."

Dianne looks around the room, then asks, "Any questions?"

After a quiet pause, Joe suggests, "Let's see how Canfield and the others are doing."

Dianne nods to Henry, "This one's all you."

Henry motions to Michael, then once they have a connection to Canfield, he sends a message to Arnold.

"Hey Henry. What the blazes is going on out there?" Arnold asks, his quick response and question surprising them all.

Henry replies, "Wow. Were you waiting at your desk?"

"Damn straight." Arnold replies, adding, "I heard from some guy, called Michael, who told me that things were pretty bad, and that you guys would be contacting me as soon as you could."

Michael shrugs, that is pretty much what he told Arnold when they made contact earlier.

Before anyone can reply Arnold continues, "Well, I gotta tell you, things are pretty ugly here too. The augment system crashed when the inner dome cracked! We've had some rioting and looting, but luckily you'd already told the public about the real situation here, so, things are probably not as bad as they could have been."

"When you say cracked? How bad is it? And what about the outer dome?" Henry asks as Arnold takes a breath.

"Every auto-fixer we send outside, stops functioning within an hour." Arnold answers. He then asks, "Does your system allow me to send pictures?"

Michael nods enthusiastically, "Yes!"

"Good," Arnold replies, "that'll be easier than explaining."

Moments later they are all staring at a series of mind-numbing images. The top of Canfield's outer dome has been blown apart, leaving gaping holes through which the inner dome can be seen. Support girders and structures lay bent, broken, and even melted, all around the rim of the dome, while massive cracks run through what remains of the outer dome.

Maggie frowns as she says, "Wow. That looks like a cracked egg! A hard-boiled one. You know, with its top lopped off."

"Yes dear," Dianne replies, then as she pats her leg, says, "Arnold, how about radiation levels? It looks like you got hit by a nuke."

"Three actually," Arnold replies, "but, luckily for us they were all air-burst, and pretty much detonated while the outer casing was still intact. If we took another hit now, I doubt the dome would hold."

Dianne cringes at the description, then asks once more, "How are radiation levels?"

Arnold checks the latest report, then says, "The radiation won't be what kills us, the cracks in the dome are expanding, and there is nothing we can do about them."

Henry grimaces as he asks, "How long?"

Arnold shrugs, "A day, a week, a month. We really don't know."

"What about the domes which are connected to Canfield?"

"They're in worse shape than us, and I've already ordered them evacuated and sealed."

Henry tilts his head as he questions, "All of them?"

Arnold explains, "Three food centers, the beach resort, and one tech dome did not survive the blasts. The rest have severe stress fractures and are being abandoned. Fortunately, casualties have been light, with less than a hundred deaths."

"We'll have to evacuate the population!" Henry states.

Joe's jaw drops as he says, "If we can't go outside, how do we do that?"

"Service tunnels!" Jerry states, surprising everyone by his answer.

Henry shakes his head as he says, "Those tunnels were only built for service lines. They're not big enough to walk down."

Jerry grins as he says, "Actually, there's a tunnel that's wide enough. It's the one which feeds Canfield its water, air, and power."

Joe narrows his eyes as he states, "So all this time you used transports, when you could have used this tunnel instead?"

Jerry hesitantly explains, "The tunnel is old, unlit, wet, and has live wires running along the walls. Secondly, it was deemed too high a security risk to allow people to use it."

Gordon looks at Joe, then says, "I didn't even know about it."

Joe presses, "Security risk?"

Henry sighs as he says, "Yes. Can you imagine what the Central Authority would have done had they found it?"

Dianne lifts her hand as she says, "Gentlemen! All that matters now, is if we can use it to get people out of Canfield and bring them here!"

Jerry takes a deep breath as he shares what he knows, "It would be dangerous, but if we were to install lighting, and keep people from touching the power cables, then, it's possible."

"Good!" Dianne exclaims. She takes a deep breath as she says, "It's going to get pretty busy here!"

"Food!" Antonio exclaims, "Doesn't Canfield grow most of our food?"

"Oh crap!" Henry states, uttering what everyone else was thinking.

Joe suddenly looks up as he suggests, "We don't need to move Aqua. We need to build a new place, somewhere where the radiation isn't a problem."

"Easier said than done!" Marco snorts.

"No, listen." Joe presses as he looks around. "Moving Aqua would take considerable effort, effort we could put into a new dome."

"We'd need three!" Jerry states, "One for food, another for water, and then one to live in."

Joe is too excited to contain his idea as he blurts out, "We start with one dome, underwater. A large one with a double, no, a triple, casing. Then, once it's done we build another, then another, with each one connected via airlocks for safety."

Gordon picks up on Joe's idea, expanding, "If we built two or three of each kind of manufacturing plant, then we'd have redundancies." He lifts his eyebrows as he glances to Dianne, adding, "And if it we're close enough, we could still keep Golem One running."

Dianne shakes her head as she looks at Jerry, "Radiation levels are too high for pipes to run along the ocean floor."

Joe grins as he says, "We tunnel under it!"

Gordon also shakes his head, "We've already heard that we need to move a considerable distance to get away from the radiation."

241

Joe grin widens as he says, "Yes, we'll probably have to move twenty or thirty kilometers away. Even if its fifty, as long as we add air locks, and allow for earthquakes, we'd be good."

Jerry looks at Antonio, and asks, "Have you ever sailed south?"

Antonio shakes his head, "We're about as south as I ever got."

"Well, about a day's travel from here, the continental shelf extends a long way out to sea, before dropping off." Jerry states with a grin, adding, "And it's no deeper than the area near here."

Dianne looks around, then proclaims, "So, the idea is to build a large, multi-layered, dome, on the continental shelf you mentioned." She pauses, then asks, "But how do we get there?"

Jerry frowns, "How did the tunnels from here to Canfield get built?"

Michael stares at his console, then as an idea comes to mind says, "Let's see what's in the database."

They stare at the screen in awe as a variety of tunneling machines are displayed, many of which are extremely long. Jerry suddenly points at the screen and exclaims, "That one!"

Henry shakes his head at Jerry, as he says, "That thing is way too small!"

Jerry points to the image as he explains, "It has a removable head, which means that as the rock wears down cutters, we can replace it. Add to this the fact that it doesn't require a special track, like many of the others we saw, and we could power it with Perkville's diesel engines!"

"If Perkville is okay." Marco interjects negatively.

Michael nods as he replies, "When I contacted them before, I was told they're okay."

Dianne looks to Jerry, then Joe, as she asks, "Do we have enough time to build these tunneling machines, dig to a new site, and build a new underwater dome, before Aqua is useless to us?"

"That's the beauty of the idea!" Jerry states with growing enthusiasm. "All we need to do, at first, is tunnel to the new area, where we install new oxygenators and water purifiers. The dome itself comes next!"

Dianne nods, "Okay. First things first. We need to evacuate Canfield. Then, get these tunneling machines built, while Aqua reroutes their intakes to buy us all as much time as they can."

"How do we evacuate Aqua?" Joe asks.

Dianne opens her mouth to answer, then shuts it again. She had assumed they would use their transports, but that is not possible anymore, not with radiation levels as high as they are.

Jerry motions to the screen, where the tunneling machine is still on display, then says, "We could install specialized docks along the tunnel, with entryways that protrude through the ocean floor."

Dianne frowns in concern as she replies, "Every time we want to *add* something, it will *add* time. And time is precious."

Gordon stares at the image on the screen, then punches his hand into his palm, shouting, "I've got it!"

Maggie jumps at the unexpected outburst, then grips Dianne's hand tightly.

Dianne glances to Maggie, concerned, then states, "Now that you've scared my little girl, would you mind sharing your epiphany?"

Gordon points as he says, "Look at the size of that thing, it's what, three meters in diameter, maybe a little bigger."

Jerry reviews the specifications, then says, "Yeah, a little over."

"Canfield's auto-fixers are smaller, pretty much round, electric driven, and programmable to do almost anything." He then grins as he states, "Especially, repairing domes and laying pipework!"

Arnold interrupts them, stating, "I think we're missing an important factor here. We lost our entire solar panel grid and are completely reliant on you for power."

Dianne replies, happy to finally have some good news, "We have a surplus of geothermal power, and always have, so that's at least something we don't have to worry about."

Henry's jaw drops as he states, "A power surplus, from geothermal energy?"

Dianne nods enthusiastically, "Yes!"

"Okay," Henry replies hesitantly, before asking, "but just where do you vent everything? There's heavy manufacturing, geothermal energy, and who knows what else, but I don't see any smoke stacks."

Instead of responding, she frowns, then shrugs.

Jerry grins as he answers, "The mountains are filled with natural caves. I recently learned that when this place was built, waste heat and steam were vented into a number of these caves, to hide the facility's true size from spy satellites."

Dianne looks around as she returns them to the topic at hand, saying, "Alright, we have a way to rescue the survivors from Canfield, but what about the other facilities?"

Jerry shrugs, "They're all connected to us by service tunnels, but, some are in disrepair, and are quite small."

Antonio adds his voice to the discussion when he says, "On the flagship, we were quite familiar with being self-sufficient, and as I see it, we'll be okay. We have power, and a way to build a tunnel to a safer region, but food would seem to be in short supply."

Dianne feels a headache forming as she replies, "Yes, food was already being rationed. I guess we'll just have to tighten our belts a little more for a while."

Antonio grins as he offers, "If you have rice, we could build rice paddies, the same way we did on the flagship. They do take a lot of water and manpower, but not much else."

Jerry nods, "Well, once we evacuate Canfield, we're going to have all the manpower we need."

Dianne relaxes a little, replying, "Good, that would help with our food shortage."

They contact Perkville, as well as the other outlying domes, and are pleased to learn that they are all in better shape than Canfield. The biggest issue is the long-term effects of radiation; thus, each community is told to prepare to evacuate.

The group talks and talks, deliberating over many of the finer details of their plans. Each time they run into a problem, they figure out a solution, then move onto the next issue. As the hours roll by, more and more points are earmarked to be figured out at a later date.

Joe stifles a yawn as he states, "This is not some project we can fall behind schedule on. The radiation is setting the deadline, and it's one we can't miss."

Gordon nods in agreement, "Let's start what we can, right now!"

"Agreed!" Dianne replies.

Jerry looks around as he offers, "I'll prepare the service tunnels for the evacuations, and get the engineers working on the new tunneling machine."

Henry offers, "I'll prepare the people of Canfield for what's next."

Michael glances at the screen, then offers, "I can help with the machine."

Gordon states, "I'll set the auto-fixers up to work in the tunnels."

Antonio nods, "And I'll get those rice fields sorted."

Marco adds, "I can help with the fields too!"

Dianne stands, then stretches her tired muscles as she says, "So, we have a plan. Let's do this!" She ends with a smile.

Plans in Motion

The days turn into weeks, with Joe becoming the unofficial go-between for Dianne and the various project leaders. He enjoys the task and begins to feel that he has a real purpose. It is a stark reminder of what is important, as opposed to when he managed imaginary money for people who thought they were rich. He keeps asking about Clarice, but the old lady never seems to be around when he is, or he is told she is sleeping and not to be disturbed.

Joe finally crosses paths with the old woman, spotting her shuffling around a corner, "Clarice, Clarice!" He calls out with urgency.

"Yes, young man." She replies, turning his way. She rests her hand on the wall for balance.

"I have been wanting to talk with you." Joe states as he walks toward her.

"Well, young man, I'm here. So, talk."

Joe smiles at her curt answer, then says, "You mentioned visiting underwater cities. I only know of Aqua."

"Oh, that was so long ago." She replies as her mind drifts off, recalling old adventures.

"Where are they?" He presses.

Clarice leans heavily against the wall, her eyes vacantly peering into the distance. Just when Joe is about to give up she startles him, "Talk to Zack! He'll remember. I just went along for the ride." Her eyes briefly sparkle as a smile crosses her lips.

"Thank you." Joe replies, disappointed.

Her eyes close briefly as she begins to slip down the wall. Her legs shake, but somehow, she manages to remain standing.

Joe looks around to see if any of the villa staff is nearby, then seeing no one, he helps her to her room. It takes them a while; he does not know where it is, and seemingly nor does Clarice.

They finally stumble into a room which looks like it belongs to her. Joe gently lays her on the bed, then as he watches her sleep he feels a sadness wash over him. He does not know why he pities her, then it suddenly dawns on him. During all this time he never thought to see if his own parents were okay. He slinks away guiltily, then promises himself to at least check on them.

Zack is much easier to get to than Clarice. Joe takes a tram directly to the council chambers, where he finds the Council leader in a deep discussion with other council members, including Dianne. He curses himself for not talking to Zack earlier; he had hoped that Clarice would have known something. The group stops talking as Joe approaches.

Dianne addresses Joe, "Yes?"

Heather gazes intently at Joe, her disdain evident all over her face, while Scott and Stephanie are more relaxed. There are three other people seated at the table, but Joe does not know who they are, nor are they introduced.

After an awkward silence, Joe nods to the council members respectfully, then says, "Zack, Clarice tells me that you know of other underwater cities."

Zack nods solemnly, then replies, "There used to be grand cities below the waves."

"What happened to them?" Joe asks, his hopes instantly dashed.

Zack looks at the other council members, then with a sad sigh, replies, "There were four cities off

248

the coast to the north of us. They were close together and about a day's travel away. It must have been around sixty years ago when it happened. No, closer to seventy."

Everyone waits, wondering what happened, as Zack seems to be wrestling in his mind with how long it has been.

"Sixty-eight years!" Zack exclaims. He looks around, suddenly realizing everyone is anxiously waiting. He continues, "There was a massive storm, the largest ever recorded. The domes were too old to cope with the powerful undercurrents, and one by one, they failed. We sent rescue teams, but all they found was a vast debris field."

Joe's jaw drops, "Is that what's washing up on the shore here?"

"Yes, mostly." Zack replies. His eyes narrow as he asks, "Now it's my turn for a question, or two."

"Of course." Joe replies.

"Dianne here keeps saying everything's going well, but I want specifics."

Heather stares at Dianne as she scathingly states, "We don't get any real information out of her!"

Dianne scowls, but remains quiet. She has found that responding to Heather simply gives the woman an excuse to rant and rave.

Joe takes a deep breath, then begins. "Canfield will have to be abandoned! But, the auto-fixers have bought us some time. The good news is that the other communities were spared the worst of the attacks and can wait until the new underwater city is ready. In the meantime, teams are working on expanding and reinforcing the tunnels between us and these communities, in preparation for the evacuations."

Zack nods as Joe pauses, and says, "What about the new city itself? How's that going?"

Joe looks up as he deliberates over how to summarize what he knows. Nodding, he begins, "The first tunneling machine is being tested, with two others being built. We are planning on two side by side tunnels, with interconnecting airlocks. Fresh water will be pumped down one side of each tunnel, with air being transferred along the other. Power and other service lines are being routed along the top, while the bottom will have a false floor, beneath which pumps are being installed to take care of any leaks."

"Such a waste!" Heather interjects, "Two tunnels will take longer than one, and require a lot of resources. We should simply build one now and the second later on."

Joe glares at her as he admonishes, "There is no simple about any of this. Relying on a single tunnel to evacuate thousands of people is pure madness."

Zack motions to Joe as he says, "Go on."

Joe takes a deep breath, then continues, "The new rice fields are proving to be more difficult than expected but should begin providing food soon enough."

Zack chuckles, "I want to hear about the new city, not the fields."

"Oh." Joe replies, realizing he has gone off tract. He exchanges a smile with Dianne, then continues. "Perkville is building new generators and designing them to fit in the tunnels. These will be installed on a massive structure on the coast near the new city and used to provide power until we get the geothermal plants operational. Once the city is self-sufficient, they'll become backup generators."

"These two tunnels. Do you expect people to walk to the city? To my understanding it's quite a ways off."

Joe excitedly answers, "No. We'll be installing a rail network, with trams running down one track, and returning along the other. But even so, it'll still take weeks to move the people of Canfield and even longer for the others."

Heather shakes her head as she states, "This is ridiculous. We should focus on improving Golem One, not trying to build a new dome. They don't last anyway."

Joe steps closer to her as he replies, "The new domes will have triple casings, for protection. Besides, we plan to return to the surface once it's safe and build a new city. The domes are only expected to be needed for one generation, but are being engineered to last centuries."

Zack stands as he looks around, "We have great confidence in your ability to keep everyone focused and on tract. Keep up the good work Joe."

Realizing he is being dismissed, Joe nods to the council members. He pauses, smiles at Dianne, then leaves.

Once more the days turn into weeks, then months as everything falls into place. The few setbacks along the way are handled quickly and efficiently. Joe continually motivates everyone with reminders that their deadline is fixed.

Deep Sea – A New Beginning

Maggie holds Joe and Dianne's hands as she skips along between them. She looks up at the dull-grey concrete high above as she says, "This is just like Aqua, only bigger."

Dianne smiles as she replies, "Yes, and this is only one dome, of many which are being built." She glances to Gordon who is heading their way, then stops.

Gordon waves as he says, "I have the controllers. The programmers have just finished testing everything."

Dianne raises her eyebrows as she questions, "I thought it was going to take a while."

Gordon shrugs as he replies, "All done in less than a year!"

Joe nods, adding, "It's a good thing too. Last I heard, radiation levels in Aqua are lethal to anyone who stays too long."

Dianne nods as she adds, "Golem's dock also has high levels of radiation, but, by the third seal, levels are virtually zero."

Maggie stares at the adults, listening. She understands what they are discussing, and wonders if they are including her on purpose.

Gordon tosses a small device to each of them, including Maggie, who beams widely. He then says, "These little units are the controllers."

Joe looks up in wonder at the huge dome overhead. It is easily twice the size of the one which covered Canfield. He plays with the controller, wondering if he should turn it on or not. He flicks the switch, and gasps. The dull-grey is gone, and instantly replaced by blue skies and puffy white clouds. He can almost feel the breeze as he stares at the horizon, where instead of seeing the edge of the dome merging with the ground, a snow tipped mountain range dominates the view, the same one visible from the resort facility where he met Henry and Miranda.

He flicks the switch off, then turns to Gordon as he asks, "So, this is our choice?"

Gordon nods as he replies, "The idea was to allow people to be more comfortable. Living under a concrete dome can cause cabin fever, and deep depression." He shrugs as he continues, "Originally, the idea was simply to allow people to enjoy the open skies, and wide countryside. It was the Central Authority who decided to use the technology to conceal the slow decay of our society."

Joe sighs, "They didn't want an uprising; they meant no harm."

Dianne and Maggie both wear specialized contact lenses and try theirs out as well.

Maggie gasps, surprised by the realism.

Gordon is also gazing around at the majestic landscape, his own implants activated.

Miranda walks up to them and smiles as she says, "I can't believe it. After all we've been through, we're safe!"

Joe fiddles with his switch as he says, "The only choice we have to make now, is do we live in the real world, or an augmented reality?"

Epilogue

Michael stares at his console, dumbfounded. He swallows hard as he turns to his colleagues, and then as a drop of sweat slides down his face, he reports, "We just got a message from the moon!"

###

I do hope you have enjoyed reading 'Augmented Reality', as much as I have enjoyed writing it.

James Jackson

Please remember to leave a review,
so that others may read your thoughts on this story.

For more information about my other works visit,
www.terranchronicles.com and
www.landsofphrey.com

To keep in touch, join the Terran Chronicles
Universe Facebook page
or follow me on Twitter @JamesAJJackson

Made in the USA
Middletown, DE
15 April 2019